He looked like a warrior, ready to do battle.

He downplayed the threat from the SUV he'd just chased off, his voice calm. But his body language said differently.

"If it's the intruder from last night, he's more of a danger."

"How so?" Krista kept the mounting panic from her voice.

"Takes someone without fear to return right after the police were called. He doesn't care who gets in his way."

This guy was persistent. Breaking in. Attacking her. Perhaps killing her if Cash hadn't arrived.

Panic threatened again but she fought it. Cash was here. Strong, capable Cash. The man she'd been fighting every step of the way.

"Thanks for being here."

"It's what I do."

"You can't possibly do this for everyone. So why me?"

He shrugged, but held her gaze, and she felt a change in him. Not the spark of attraction that clearly existed between them. Something softer. Something that made her forget the bomber.

"I can't put my finger on it, but I know you need me." His voice was low and husky.

The word *trustworthy* came to mind. A man of honor. Could she really believe he was everything he seemed to be... even if he discovered who she really was?

Susan Sleeman is a bestselling author of inspirational and clean-read romantic suspense books and mysteries. Awards include RT Reviewers' Choice Best Book for *Thread of Suspicion*; *No Way Out* and *The Christmas Witness* were finalists for the Daphne du Maurier Award for Excellence. She's had the pleasure of living in nine states and currently lives in Oregon. To learn more about Susan visit her website at susansleeman.com.

Books by Susan Sleeman

Love Inspired Suspense

High-Stakes Inheritance
Behind the Badge
The Christmas Witness
Holiday Defenders
"Special Ops Christmas"

The Justice Agency

Double Exposure
Dead Wrong
No Way Out
Thread of Suspicion
Dark Tide

First Responders

Silent Night Standoff
Explosive Alliance

Visit the Author Profile page at Harlequin.com for more titles.

EXPLOSIVE
ALLIANCE

SUSAN SLEEMAN

HARLEQUIN® LOVE INSPIRED® SUSPENSE

LOVE INSPIRED BOOKS

ISBN-13: 978-0-373-67678-1

Explosive Alliance

And the peace of God, which transcends all understanding,
will guard your hearts and your minds in Christ Jesus.
–*Philippians* 4:7

For the many law enforcement bomb squads and military disposal technicians who risk their lives on a daily basis to rid our world of dangerous explosives. It takes a special person to do this job, and I hope I honor them in the way I have portrayed bomb tech Cash Dixon.

ONE

Murderer!

The word hung in the soggy air.

Krista Curry could feel it. Taste it. Smell it.

She hunched forward, hiding her face and holding her breath, waiting for someone in the crowd to recognize her. To shout out the horrific title she'd been branded with after her husband, Toby, was murdered four years ago.

She shifted on the hard stadium chair. Risked a quick glance around Providence Park's open-air stadium. Rain flooded from dusky skies, the seats glistening, the players soaked as they slogged over a field shadowed with whispery swatches of fog.

"Watch the net." Her grandfather's shout mingled with the crowd's cheers for the Portland Timbers. His cheeks were rosy from the cold, the pure joy of the sport widening his smile that was often marred from battling cancer.

Krista's heart creased with concern for him. She didn't know if he'd beat stage three cancer or how many more joyful days he'd have. She'd do anything for him. Including risking recognition and someone calling her out in public so he could attend the soccer match.

Oh, Opa. Her precious Opa.

She loved everything about him, including his insistence that she use the informal German name for grandfather. He was the one man she could count on. The man who'd helped her survive the loss of her mother. Who'd stood by her when her father had gone to prison for murder. Who'd believed in her when she'd been accused of killing Toby.

She couldn't lose him to cancer. She just couldn't.

"Did you see that save, Liebchen?" he asked excitedly, using his pet name that meant sweetheart. He placed a hand on her knee. She jumped, immediately regretting her startled response when concern wiped away his joy.

He eyed her for a long, uncomfortable moment. "What is going on in that mind that has you wound as tight as a spring?"

"Nothing that's worth taking you away from your game."

He watched her for another second before turning back to the match. The Timbers scored a goal. He whooped loudly. He suddenly clutched his neck and coughed, cleared his throat and coughed harder. He gasped for air, his chest heaving with the effort.

She grabbed his water only to discover she'd

kicked the cup over. She swirled the container, grateful to find a small amount of liquid still in the bottom. He quickly gulped it down, then cleared his throat hard.

"Better?" she asked.

He sighed out a long breath. "Better."

She took the cup. "If I go fill this, will you be okay by yourself?"

"I am not one of the preschoolers in your class, you know." His feisty attitude returned, along with his fierce sense of independence. The same independence she'd fought since she'd come back to Portland weeks ago to care for him. The chemo treatments left him more helpless than he'd admit, and he continued to make decisions that weren't always in his best interest. Coming to the match was a perfect example. Now he needed water to stay hydrated and silence his cough.

"I'll be right back." She slipped around his feet and avoided making eye contact with anyone. She put one foot in front of the other on the slick concrete. Down the stairs. Quickly toward the Mezzanine Terrace. Praying for anonymity.

Feeling eyes on her, she raised her head. Inch by inch, she scanned the area ahead. A uniformed deputy leaned against the railing, his focus on her.

No. Oh, no. Did he recognize her? Did he know about Toby's murder—about the accusations? That even though the police had never brought formal charges, she hadn't been fully cleared?

Or maybe he'd simply noticed her jumpy behavior and suspected she was up to something. The last thing she needed or wanted was for a cop to start questioning her.

He caught her studying him and smiled. A sizzling, I'm-all-that kind of smile. A clear look of interest burned in his eyes. He didn't know who she was. This was a simple case of a man interested in a woman. In her. It was there in his eyes. There in his body turned toward her. Anticipation saturated his expression and he didn't try to hide it. Her heart gave a kick. Warning bells followed, telling her to look away, but she couldn't manage it.

She suddenly realized she was staring and dropped her gaze to the walkway to take the last few steps without falling.

She heard him chuckle before he said, "Evening, ma'am."

His lazy, Southern drawl took her by surprise, bringing her eyes back up. She caught a quick look at his name tag—Deputy Cash Dixon—before the heat of a blush crept up her face.

"You look a bit flustered," he went on. "Anything I can help you with?"

Ugh! He knew why she was flustered. He was teasing her.

She held up the empty cup and stepped past him.

Another chuckle followed her into the concourse, but she tuned him out and retrieved the water. On the return trip, she felt his focus on her again but refused to let him bait her into looking his way and hurried up the stairs. As she neared her row, the man seated to her left got up and moved into the aisle, leaving his backpack behind.

"Your pack," she called out and pointed at it, but he didn't look up.

She stepped in front of him to get his attention.

His head jerked up, his steely-gray eyes dark with anger meeting hers. He shoved his hands into his sweatshirt pocket, then blinked in surprise.

"Sorry to bother you," she said, trying not to wilt under his continued study. "But you left your backpack."

His eyes lingered for long, tense moments before he brushed by her and jogged down the stairs.

"So much for trying to be a good citizen," she mumbled and stepped past Opa. "Did you see that guy who just left?"

Opa shook his head, but kept his attention on the game. "He blocked my view for a few seconds, but I didn't actually look at him. Why?"

"He left his backpack. When I told him about it, he got mad."

"Odd," Opa said absently, his focus still pinned on the field.

Krista handed the water to Opa and looked at the pack a few seats away. That unsettled feeling returned.

Stop it, Krista. What did she think was in the pack, a bomb?

Ha! The guy was rude, maybe a bit creepy, but that didn't make him some lunatic leaving a bomb behind. He'd likely had too much to drink, needed to use the restroom and would be right back. That's why he didn't take her concern seriously.

She ignored the fact that there weren't any empty cups by his seat and forced her attention on to the game. Not that she knew anything about football, as Opa called it, other than it involved a ball with two nets and Opa loved it. She tried to get into the game, but the backpack kept nagging at her, and she continued to check her watch. The man had been gone for fifteen minutes. Far too long for a trip to the bathroom or snack bar when long lines weren't likely due to tonight's low attendance.

Her gaze slid back to the pack.

Should she check it out? With all the craziness going on in the world today, could she afford not to check it out?

She glanced down the stairs to confirm the guy wasn't returning, then slid over to the pack. Once a vivid blue, it was now worn and dingy gray. She checked for the owner one last time, then pulled the zipper and spread it open.

A cell phone lay on a stack of red blocks. Next to it, large neon-green numbers on a timer counted down from twenty-seven minutes fifty seconds. It was strapped to the bricks resembling modeling clay with wires leading to the stack.

Timer. Bricks. Wires.

"Bo—" she started to shout, then realized what yelling "bomb" would do to nearby spectators.

A bomb! It's really a bomb. What should she do?

She and Opa didn't have cell phones, so she couldn't call 911. So then what?

Think, Krista, think.

The numerals kept flashing their countdown— taunting her.

Twenty-five minutes ten seconds. Nine. Eight.

Panic crawled up her spine.

No, no, no!

Why had she waited so long to look? How should she handle this?

Deputy Cash Dixon, the name barreled into her brain. She had to alert him.

She started to rise. Caught sight of Opa. In his fragile state, if she took him with her, it would take a long time to climb down the stairs. Precious minutes would be wasted before the bomb squad could be notified. She had no choice. She'd have to leave him sitting in his seat.

Here. Near a bomb.

She couldn't do that to her Opa.

You have to or all of these people could die. Go! Now!

She'd bring the deputy up here, leave this situation in his hands and guide Opa to the exit. She had enough time. *If* she hurried.

Her stomach threatening to revolt, she gently closed the flaps on the pack from prying eyes and jumped to her feet.

"I'll be right back, Opa." She forced the words over a lump in her throat.

"Okay." He didn't look up.

"I love you." She hoped it wouldn't be the last time she ever said these words to him.

His perceptive gaze met hers. "What's wrong, Liebchen?"

"Nothing." She offered him a wobbly smile, then jogged down the stairs to discover Cash Dixon now leaned against the restaurant wall, that casual pose still in place. Her confidence in him evaporated.

Could he handle this? This man who seemed to excel in flirting? Was he just a pretty face, or was he cool and calm under pressure? Steady? Trustworthy?

Because he needed to be. Desperately needed to be, if he was going to stop this bomb from exploding and bringing the building down around them.

TWO

Rent-a-cop duty.

Could Cash sink any lower on the boredom scale? He didn't usually go in for security duty, but his buddy's wife was having a baby and his buddy needed someone to cover at the last minute. Ninety minutes into the job, he was regretting his decision to help.

He glanced at his solid titanium watch he'd worn on countless Delta Force missions.

Now *that* was an exciting job.

There was nothing more thrilling than serving on the army's elite tier-one Special Ops team. Fast-roping down to free a hostage. Night jumps and rock climbs to raid insurgent groups in Afghanistan. Diving into dark, murky waters.

Man, he missed it. Missed it all. The team. The camaraderie. Working with guys who really got him. His life hadn't been the same since a friendly bomb had gone astray, taking out his whole team. Why he'd survived, he had no idea, even after eighteen months.

Stop, he warned himself. Standing here brooding wouldn't help him figure it out. He needed to keep busy.

He searched the crowd, looking for someone whose chops he could bust. He spotted the woman who'd brushed past him a few minutes ago to retrieve a cup of water charging down the steps.

Good. Just the distraction he was looking for. A particularly beautiful one at that. He loved the way she'd blushed when he'd flirted with her. Wasn't often these days that he ran into a woman exhibiting such innocence.

She hit the landing and ran toward him, skidding to a stop in front of him. Eyes the color of his army dress blues were dark with worry, sending a curl of apprehension into his gut.

"I need your help." She panted to catch her breath. "There's a…" She paused to look around, then drew him away from a man standing nearby.

She leaned close to Cash's ear. He caught a faint whiff of vanilla and another appealing spice he couldn't identify.

"There's a bomb," she whispered, her breath warm on his skin.

He pulled back. "Don't even kid about that, ma'am."

"I'm not kidding." Full lips drew down in a scowl as her gaze continued to dart around.

"What's your name, ma'am?"

"Krista Curry."

"Well, Krista, why don't you tell me what you

saw?" It was very unlikely she'd actually seen a bomb, but whatever she'd witnessed had clearly upset her and he needed to take it seriously.

"It's by my seat," she said. "A guy got up and left his backpack. There's a cell phone inside with a timer attached to a bunch of red bricks. It's counting down. It had twenty-five minutes on it. Now it must be closer to twenty." She grabbed his arm in a viselike grip. "Please, we can't waste any time."

Something in her desperate plea made him believe her enough to agree to check out the so-called device. "Show me."

She led him toward the aisle and gestured at the upper section. "See the older man seated in the second row from the top? That's my grandfather. The backpack is six seats to his left. By that big girder."

He looked at the upper section, saw a gray-haired man sitting at the aisle, intent on the game.

"Wait. That woman." Krista wiggled her finger at a stick-thin woman climbing over a seat. "Looks like she's spotted the backpack. She's going to open it just like I did. She might... Oh, no."

He saw the woman, but he couldn't see the backpack. Krista grabbed his arm again. "We need to get up there before she does something stupid."

The woman fumbled around at her feet. She looked up, her gaze wild and unfocused.

"Bomb!" she screamed and charged for the aisle. "There's a bomb in that backpack. Only fifteen minutes on the timer. Run! Everybody run!" She catapulted over the old man's legs, nearly lost her balance but recovered to run down the steps, waving her arms and inciting the crowd. "Bomb! There's a bomb! Go!"

People fled toward the exits in a stampede. Cash had to restore order before they trampled each other. At least attendance was down due to the rain, and he had a chance of calming them down.

"C'mon, people!" He held up his hands. "This is someone's bad idea of a joke, but just to be safe, let's clear the area in an orderly fashion."

"It's no joke—I saw it," the woman shouted, her eyes so terrified Cash figured she wasn't making it up, but the device could still be a dummy left to cause a riot.

"I've got to get to Opa!" Krista darted toward the steps.

Cash ran after her and jerked her into an empty aisle moments before the fleeing mob reached them. "You can't go up there. They'll trample you."

She tried to wrench free. "But my grandfather needs me. I can't leave him alone."

The last thing Cash wanted was for another person to lose their life on his watch so he tightened his hold while he reported the situation over his radio. He ordered the security team to cease use of their radios from this point forward. He'd take no chance of the radio signal setting off the bomb if it was real. He'd make one more call to the team leader for the First Response Squad—the tactical team Cash served on. The six-person squad was created to deal with emergency situations just like this one and would be the first to respond. Once he notified them, he'd go radio silent, too.

"Let. Me. Go!" Krista's volume escalated with each word.

"I can't."

"Please." Her eyes darted around as if she might lose it any second. "I have to help him. I have to."

She jerked harder. Cash let go of his radio to catch her chin, forcing her to make eye contact. "Calm down, Krista. If you promise to stay right here, I'll take care of your gramps."

She stopped thrashing and eyed him suspiciously. "Really? You'll get him out of here?"

After I get a look at that bomb and, if it's legit, disarm it if I can. Thankfully, he was on duty tonight. His buddy Neil was a great guy, but he wasn't a bomb expert. Cash had years of experience disarming explosives in the military and another year as the FRS bomb tech.

He looked around for another officer to hand Krista off to but found no one. "I'll go, but you have to stay here. Right here on this spot. No moving at all. Promise?"

She nodded unreservedly.

He hoped she was sincere and wasn't playing him. "I mean it. If I look back down here and see you've moved at all, I won't follow through."

"You'd leave him?"

No, but you don't need to know that. "If you force me to."

"I won't move. I promise. Just go. Now! Hurry!"

Cash released her arm and surveyed the chaos as he formed a quick game plan. With crazed people flooding down the aisle, he'd have to climb over seats to reach the top, then hope the crowd had thinned enough, allowing him to shoot across the aisle to the bomb.

He started over the seats. One by one. Up. Higher. Toward the bomb.

"Be careful, Deputy," Krista called out.

He felt his stride falter. Not for long. The briefest of moments, really, but long enough for the memory of his fallen teammates to come rushing back.

Stow it, man. Or these people could pay the price for your distraction. Keep calm. In control. Step by step. Work through it.

He could do this. He *had* to do this. If the bomb was real, it was up to him—him alone—to disarm the device. With fifteen minutes on the timer, neither his squad nor the Metropolitan Explosives Disposal Unit could arrive on time.

If he even had the fifteen minutes to get this done.

More likely he had less.

Putting a cell phone on the bomb said the bomber planned to detonate via a phone call and the timer was likely a fallback. A simple ring of the phone and the bomb could go off in a split second, killing everyone in the blast radius.

He upped his speed, reaching the top tier. He looked for a break in the crowd. A cold bead of sweat dampening his forehead, he shot across the aisle, found the backpack and gently opened it. The sight that greeted him sent his heart plummeting.

He shone his flashlight into the pack, following the detonator wire from the timer now at twelve minutes to demolition blocks stacked neatly inside.

He let out a low whistle, and a sinking feeling in the pit of his stomach followed.

There was nothing fake about this bomb. Nothing at all.

THREE

"No-o-o-o!" Raw fear uncoiled in Krista's stomach. "Don't mess with it. Opa first. Please!" Her words came from deep in her gut, but there was no chance Cash could hear her over the crowd.

Was he trying to be a hero? Trying to disarm the bomb himself instead of waiting for a trained technician?

Of course he was. He was a hotheaded cop like the ones who'd railroaded her toward a murder rap. And she'd trusted him. Stupidly. She was the worst kind of granddaughter. She'd left Opa a stone's throw from a bomb, then trusted the wrong person again.

You're a fool, Krista.

She was about to charge up there, but Cash turned and headed in Opa's direction. He squatted in front of him. They talked, Opa responding with his usual animated gesturing. Cash patted Opa's hand then stood and looked away. Krista waited for Opa to get up, but he sat there watching Cash walk toward the bomb.

What?

"No! What're you doing?" she screamed.

He took a tool from his pocket and bent over the bomb. He *was* going to try to disarm it and leave Opa all alone.

Fear skittered down Krista's spine. She couldn't stand there any longer and leave her grandfather in extreme peril. She took off, following the trail Cash had left behind, pushing through people like a snowplow. She wouldn't stop. No matter what. She was going up to Opa's seat even if the crowd trampled her to death.

Adrenaline raced through Cash's veins, leaving him light-headed for a moment. He took in a calming breath. Blew it out and replayed his radio conversation with Jake, the FRS leader. The team had an ETA of ten minutes, but once they arrived, they still would have to fight through the crowd streaming out of the stadium.

Translated, Cash was on his own.

So did he move the bomb? Disarm it? Jake had told Cash to use his gut feeling. *His gut, right.* His gut couldn't be trusted. Afghanistan proved that.

He stared at the bomb for a moment. Thinking. Evaluating. His best option was to get the device away from people. Center field would be good, but safely moving through the crowd while carrying a bomb would be problematic. So then what?

He checked the timer.

08:29.

08:28.

08:27.

He had to act. Move it or disarm it, which was less risky? He just didn't know. He used to be so decisive. Until the loss of his team.

He glanced around, assessing the number of people still in the blast radius, and saw Krista urgently climbing over seats to get to her grandfather.

Otto seemed like a fine gentleman. He'd thanked Cash for risking his life to disarm the bomb and for his willingness to sacrifice himself for others, then told him to go ahead with his job and not worry about him. He was counting on Cash to make the right decision. So was Krista. So were all the people in the stadium.

A lump formed in Cash's throat, but he wouldn't disappoint them.

He knew what he had to do. He flipped open his Leatherman and went to work on the antiremoval device. Each movement calculated. Precise.

The noise of the crowd. The announcer. The sounds of other officers who'd responded, all fading into the background. It was just him and the device. And the timer.

He wasn't one for praying. Not since answers to his questions about the loss of his former team remained unanswered, but if any situation called for hope and prayer, this one did.

He sent up a quick request to keep everyone

safe. To make his movements sure and true. He took a deep breath, held it and decisively disconnected the device.

With no time to spare, he moved on to the detonator, carefully pulling it from the Semtex and moving it well away from the explosives. The timer continued counting down, but with the detonator removed, it no longer mattered.

"Done!" he called out, then wiped perspiration from his forehead.

Before he could celebrate, in his peripheral vision he caught someone quickly advancing toward him. He was instantly on alert again.

He jerked around, his hand flying to his gun.

Krista raced across the now-deserted aisle.

"What're you doing?" She rushed up to him, her eyes immediately going to the backpack. "The timer is almost down to zero and you promised to get Opa out of here. Let's hurry. Now!"

He opened his mouth to tell her that he'd disarmed the bomb, but she flew at him and pounded his chest. He grabbed her hands. They were icy cold and trembling. "We've got to go. Now! Help us. Please."

"Krista," Otto said calmly from behind them.

Cash continued to clutch her hands as she looked over her shoulder at her grandfather. "Opa, we have to go."

"But Cash is a bomb technician. He has disarmed the bomb. There is no longer any danger."

She whirled on Cash. "Why didn't you tell me?"

"I tried to."

She jerked her hands free, looking torn between aggravation with him and relief that her grandfather was safe. She made quite a sight, her cheeks flushed and her eyes bright. Her fiery personality contrasted with her elegant, tailored clothing, which Cash bet cost a pretty penny. Not that he had much experience with such things from his low-income upbringing, but he knew quality when he saw it.

"Let me arrange for someone to stand watch on the backpack, and I'll assist you with helping Otto down the stairs," he offered.

"I don't need your help." She turned away. "Let's get you up, Opa."

"I'm feeling tired," Otto said, a smile in his voice. "I think it would be better to wait for the nice young man to help us."

She jerked around to look at Cash again, her frustration with waiting for him rampant in her expression.

Cash stifled a snort and radioed for an officer. She watched him, her jaw jutted out in defiance. She was a tenacious little thing, battling for her grandfather at all costs, a trait Cash admired. By the time the officer arrived and Cash had given him instructions, she had Opa on his feet.

He was clearly in poor health, and today's scare

had likely rattled him more than he was willing to admit. Cash would do his best to help Otto relax.

Cash took the older man's elbow and winked at him. "Let me know if you catch the eye of a pretty lady. I'll let go so we don't ruin your cred as a ladies' man."

Otto shook with laughter. "I like you, Cash Dixon."

Krista glared at him. It was obvious *she* didn't like him. Not the least little bit. No skin off his nose. He was hardly boyfriend material right now. The jury was still out on whether he'd ever be again.

They slowly worked their way toward the main concourse. Otto chatted all the way down, his attitude remarkably cheerful.

Around the corner, Cash spotted the First Response Squad barreling up the ramp. Five strong, they wore uniforms of black tactical pants and black collared knit shirts. Kevlar vests covered with intricate FRS logos on their chests.

"Late to the party, I see," Cash joked, though he was glad to see them.

Jake marched up to Cash. "We good?"

"Yeah. The device is disarmed. I've put an officer on the backpack. When MEDU arrives they can dispose of the Semtex."

"Good job, man." Jake clapped Cash on the back.

Brady Owens, whose shaggy blond hair made

him look like a surfer instead of a sniper, socked Cash in the arm. "When the building didn't blow up on schedule, we figured you had things under control."

"Yeah, man." Archer Reed, a team negotiator and the only member of the group taller than Cash, grinned. "We're glad you didn't go boom."

Despite the obvious sarcasm, Cash knew both men were sincerely relieved that he was all right.

Negotiator Skyler Brennan, small for a law enforcement officer, with fiery red hair, stepped forward. Her size often had people underestimating her strength and determination, but she was one of the strongest women Cash had ever met. She lifted her arms to give him a hug.

He wasn't about to let anyone hug him on the job. He stepped back, and she looked hurt.

"Don't be rude, Cash Dixon," EMT Darcie Stevens chastised. The self-professed mom of the group, she kept everyone in line.

A job Cash could never do. Making a bunch of adrenaline junkies mind their manners and play nice together was a thankless job. But Darcie did it well. Most of the time anyway. When she wasn't trying to get all the guys to express their feelings. That was just plain annoying.

"Don't worry, Darcie," Skyler said. "I get it. Cash's on duty. He can't possibly let people think he's less than a macho alpha male." She grinned at Cash, then turned her attention to Krista. "When

Cash called this in, he told us how well you handled discovering the bomb. Most people would've screamed or fainted."

Krista shot Cash a surprised look.

He shrugged it off.

"Don't mind him." Skyler wrinkled her nose at Cash. "He doesn't like people to see it, but he's a real softy."

Cash groaned. "Maybe we should keep the focus on Krista, not me."

"My Krista is an amazing woman," Otto said fondly. "I'm glad for others to see this, as well."

Jake cast an intimidating look at Otto. "And you are?"

"I am her very proud grandfather, Otto Schiffer." Otto puffed out his chest.

"A brave man in his own right." Cash relayed how Otto had been willing to give up his life so Cash could disarm the bomb instead of helping Otto exit the arena.

A flush colored Otto's face, his silvery beard now more pronounced. "It wasn't anything that anyone else wouldn't do."

"If you don't mind, can we end this praise fest and move things along?" Brady tapped his foot on the concrete.

He was constantly in motion, a field of energy always buzzing around him, but he had a laid-back, carefree attitude. Cash was more deliberate. Moved slower. Thought things through and weighed the consequences. Still, as a former Marine Scout Sniper, Brady's past military experience made him the person Cash connected with most on the team, despite their different personalities.

"For once I agree with your need for speed, Brady." Jake changed his focus to Krista. "The sooner we get your statement, the sooner we can catch our bomber."

"Wait, what?" Brady swiveled to face Jake. "We're staying to take her statement?"

Cash seconded the question. The FRS was needed in the moment of crisis to take care of the immediate danger. They were rarely involved in the subsequent investigation other than holding a debriefing to evaluate and improve their performance for the next incident.

"With the gravity of this situation, the higher-ups have already decided the county will form a joint task force with the city. Skyler will take lead for County." Jake turned to Krista. "In addition to Skyler's duties as a negotiator on our team, she's also a detective with the county's Special Investigation Unit. She's asked us to sit in while she takes your statement."

Darcie lifted her medical bag. "After I give them a quick evaluation."

"The restaurant looks deserted. We can meet in there." Jake took off, his long strides carrying him swiftly down the empty corridor.

The team followed like ducklings after their mama, Krista and Otto trailing them. Cash chose to hang back for a few seconds to clear his mind. Still, he let his gaze track Krista. He'd never admit it to anyone, but he was glad he didn't have to say goodbye to her just yet.

Brady turned back and eyed Cash.

Right. Get moving before everyone starts asking questions.

"Dude." Brady slugged Cash again. "You're practically drooling. Not that I blame you. She's a real looker. But you'd better get your head together before Jake notices."

Cash laughed, pretending to blow off Brady's comment.

Brady was right—Krista was a real looker. But what really attracted him was the care and concern she exhibited for her grandfather. After Cash's parents had died when he was eight and he'd been passed around from home to home, he could appreciate the obvious love they both shared.

Still, he wouldn't let this interest in her distract him. Not now. Not when his help was needed to locate this very dangerous bomber before he struck again.

FOUR

Krista helped Opa find a seat in the restaurant as the First Response Squad connected tables, allowing the group to sit together.

What a team.

Six people. Calm, efficient and quick to move. Intimidating, really. Very intimidating.

Except for the EMT, Darcie. Tall and thin with auburn hair in a ponytail, Darcie's warm, motherly attributes shone through as she squatted in front of Krista and took her vital signs. Everything about Darcie exuded compassion and friendliness.

Maybe her kindness proved that this team was different from the detectives investigating Toby's murder. Would they actually be kind to her instead of falsely accusing her? Trashing her name in the media and ruining her life, leaving her no choice but to flee from Portland?

Could she be lucky enough to stumble upon decent cops who believed in someone's innocence until proven guilty?

Like their leader, Jake Marsh. Was he a good guy? He oozed strength and seemed to analyze every step before acting. Exactly what Krista would expect from a leader. At the same time, he didn't pressure Darcie to finish her exam so they could start the questioning. A good balance for the deputies who counted on him, Krista supposed.

He talked with Brady, who she'd gathered from their chatter held the position of sniper. Solidly built, he had a carefree smile and laid-back look, but he bounced around the room like a Super Ball. The team negotiator named Archer was long, lean and intense, his gaze watchful all the time. As if he was trying to figure out what made people tick. Skyler, who was about Krista's height, stood next to him. She carried herself with a self-assurance that warned Krista to be careful around her.

And Cash? The man she tried not to look at? She didn't know what to make of him.

Over six feet with a muscular build, he had dark hair, a wide jaw and intense eyes that lightened up only when he smiled. He was a fine-looking man, there was no disputing that. One most women would jump at a chance to date. But not her. She'd had no interest in dating since she'd discovered Toby had lied to her.

Cash looked up and caught her watching him. A slow smile crept across his face, his eyes glinting with amusement as if he could read her mind. She felt her face heat up again and jerked her gaze back to Darcie.

Darcie shot a curious look at Cash, then

frowned up at Krista. "Your pulse and blood pressure are good, but shock can sometimes be delayed." She hung her stethoscope around her neck. "The others will focus on getting as much information from you as possible to have a better chance at finding the bomber. Not me. I'll keep an eye on you during the interview to be sure you're handling this okay. If at any time you need a break, ask for one."

"I will."

Darcie scooted over to Opa and took his pulse.

Skyler joined them and handed out bottles of water. "It's important to stay hydrated, too."

"Thank you." Krista's stomach was a tight knot. She couldn't imagine putting anything, even water, in it, but nerves had left her mouth dry. She took a long pull on the bottle.

"This isn't our first crisis situation so we understand what you're going through." Skyler smiled, yet Krista could see questions lurking in her eyes.

"I'd appreciate it if you could continue monitoring Opa's medical condition."

"Opa?" Skyler asked.

"Means grandfather in German." Krista peered at Opa, who was greedily drinking from the bottle while Darcie strapped the blood pressure cuff on his arm. "He's been undergoing chemo treatments and—"

"And she worries too much about me." He waved off Krista's concern. "Please don't go to any trouble for me. I dare say I am doing better than my Liebchen here."

Krista patted his knee. "They can look after both of us."

Darcie ripped the Velcro cuff from Opa's arm and stood. "If you start to feel dizzy or short of breath, don't try to be a hero. Tell me right away."

Opa nodded and Darcie turned. "We're good to go, Jake."

His clipped nod seemed to fit his no-nonsense personality. "If everyone will join us at the table, we'll get started."

Krista helped Opa to his feet and, for once, he didn't shrug off her help but leaned heavily on her arm. Which troubled Krista more than if he'd tried to move on his own. This day was taking a toll on him, and she needed to get him home as soon as possible.

She settled him in a chair near the head of the table, deposited their jackets on another chair and sat next to him, far away from Cash Dixon. He remained standing, resting a shoulder against a window overlooking the midfield section of the stadium.

Looking out past him, she saw powerful lights illuminating the empty field. The bomb still sat high in the stands and cops swarmed around the area, probably looking for anything that could help them track the bomber. That man. That creep who'd tried to kill children. Families. Opa.

And she'd seen him. Up close and personal—could identify him.

Would he realize that and try to find her to silence her?

A shudder started at Krista's head and worked over her body. She willed away memories of the bomber's cold eyes. Willed away her fear of him coming after her and clamped her hands together under the table. Opa needed her to stay strong and get through this quickly to take him home.

She focused on Jake, who stood at the head of the table, carefully appraising her. She tried not to shrink back from the intensity of his expression. Her past experience with police officers told her he'd likely take it to mean she was hiding something so she smiled and forced herself to relax taut muscles in her shoulders.

He didn't return her smile, but sat on the corner of the table, his determined gaze never leaving her. "Go ahead and tell us what happened today. Start with your arrival at the field and really think about anything unusual you might've seen." He turned his focus to Opa, and Krista resisted sighing with relief. "If you can add anything along the way, Mr. Schiffer, feel free to jump in."

"Please." He waved a hand. "Stop with this Mr. Schiffer business. It's Otto."

"Okay, Otto." A tight-lipped smile briefly lifted the corner of Jake's mouth, but it disappeared when he looked at Krista again. "Go ahead, Ms. Curry."

Unlike Opa, Krista didn't ask him to call her by her first name. Formality would make it feel less personal should they fire accusations at her later. It would also continue to remind them of her last name. A name she'd had to assume after the press had vilified her. A name that should help conceal a connection to Toby and leave her past in the past.

"We didn't want to battle traffic so we arrived on the MAX train," she said, reminding herself to stick to facts that couldn't be misconstrued and later turned against her. "We entered through Gate 2. After stopping at a water fountain to fill our cup, we went straight to our seats."

Skyler pulled a notepad from her backpack. "Was the bomber in his seat when you arrived?"

Was he?

Krista squeezed her eyes shut, trying to force away the terror of the final moments to remember the beginning. Entering the stadium. Climbing the stairs as quickly as she could with Opa. Watching her feet so no one had the chance to get a good look at her face and recognize her. Settling into her seat. Keeping her head down—way down—until the match started.

Not something she'd tell the team eyeing her. The minute they learned she remained a suspect in a murder investigation was the minute they'd brand her a criminal and start thinking she could be involved in this incident, too.

She glanced at Opa. "I don't remember if he was there. Do you?"

"I only had eyes for my Timbers, but he must have been in his seat. I would have noticed if he arrived after us and got between me and my football game."

"Makes sense." Skyler flipped the page in her notebook. "What time did you arrive?"

"I didn't look at the clock." Krista took a quick sip of water. "But I'd guess it was about ten minutes before the match started."

"I concur," Opa added.

Skyler jotted a note, then looked up. "What happened after you took your seats?"

Krista ran through the events in her mind and nothing except her worry of being recognized stood out. "The match started, and it was just the usual things you'd expect. Vendors. People coming and going."

Skyler's eyes bored into Krista. "When did you first notice the man who left the backpack?"

Krista forced herself to meet Skyler's intimidating gaze. "I accidently spilled Opa's water. When he started coughing, I went down to the mezzanine to get more."

"That's when I first saw you," Cash said with no inflection in his tone to give away his thoughts.

She nodded as the memory of his intense study

and blatant flirtation made her uneasy. She took a quick cleansing breath before she blushed again and drew attention to the attraction between them, then looked Cash straight in the eye. "Then maybe you saw me when I returned, too."

"I saw you," he said, and this time, she saw a flicker of amusement in his eyes.

So the flirting continues. Great.

Despite the desire to look away, Krista kept her focus on him. "That's when I bumped into the bomber, which means you saw him, too."

"Ah…" The flicker in his eyes turned to full-bloom amusement. "I wasn't exactly focusing on the bomber."

Brady snorted. "I could've told you that."

Cash crossed his arms, the taut muscles flexing. He fired a testy look at Brady.

Brady laughed. "Hey, man, it would've been great if you'd seen the guy, but no one blames you for looking at Krista instead of an ugly old bomber."

Chuckles traveled around the table but did nothing to alleviate Krista's tension.

Skyler was the only team member who didn't seem amused. "You bumped into the bomber?"

Krista nodded. "He was leaving as I was returning from the water fountain. I noticed he'd left his backpack, but when I tried to tell him, he ignored me and kept going. So I stepped in his path to stop him. He stared at me for a minute, then brushed past me."

"Why didn't you tell me, Liebchen?" Opa asked, sounding hurt.

"I thought he was just a rude man, and I love you, Opa, but I can't tell you about every rude man I encounter." She gave Cash a pointed look. "I figured he was headed to the bathroom and would come back for his pack later, so I took my seat. After he didn't return in fifteen minutes, I looked in the pack. I saw the bomb and remembered Deputy Dixon. I went to tell him about it. He agreed to look at the backpack."

Cash pushed off the window and planted his feet. "That's when the other woman saw the bomb and her warning sent everyone into panic mode. Krista wanted to go after Otto, but she agreed to let me go instead. I scoped out the bomb and rendered it safe."

Skyler's pen hovered over her notebook as she stared at Krista. "Now would be a good time to give us a physical description of the bomber."

Images of the creep slunk through her mind. Her hands trembled. She clenched them harder while dredging up the nerve to speak of him.

"Are you all right, Ms. Curry?" Darcie asked.

No. She doubted she'd be all right for a very long time. But she wanted this monster caught, so she forced herself back to the moment in the aisle. "He's Caucasian. Maybe six feet. Thin. I'd say in his late twenties. He wore jeans and a green Timbers sweatshirt with the hood up. I saw a bit of black hair on his forehead. The rest was hidden. His face is long with a pointed chin. His eyes are grayish blue." Memories of the hatred in his eyes sent a cold chill through her body. "His eyes were mean. Extremely mean." She shook her head. "Maybe I should've known he planned to kill people…all of us. If I had done more to stop him, he might not be free to try again."

"Don't blame yourself, Liebchen." Opa's papery-soft hand settled over hers and she clung to him. "You couldn't have known."

"It sounds like you saw him well enough to help our sketch artist render an accurate drawing," Skyler said. "Are you willing to meet with him?"

Krista nodded. "I'll never forget his face. Never."

"I'll set something up for tomorrow. Is there a time that's best for you?"

"I teach preschool and the kids need me there. I have two sessions a day. I start at seven and get off at four."

Skyler frowned. "I'd rather not wait an entire day. What about a lunch break? Could we do it then?"

"Yes, if your artist comes to the preschool at noon."

"I'll make sure it happens." Skyler pulled her

gaze from Krista for the first time since the questioning had begun. "Anyone else have questions?"

Brady looked right at Krista, not the least bit uncomfortable pinning her with a hard stare. "We wouldn't be doing our jobs if we didn't at least ask Ms. Curry if she's involved in this."

Here it comes. The accusations.

Opa grasped his chest. "Och, not my Krista. She'd never do a thing like this. Don't you have security cameras that caught our arrival? If so, you can see for yourself that she carried no backpack."

"To get through security she would have had to stow the pack with the bomb in advance," Jake said.

She crossed her arms. "How could I have gotten materials in here? I have no access."

"But a friend might." Skyler watched Krista carefully, measuring, weighing.

"I just returned to Portland two weeks ago. After being gone for four years, I know few people in town, let alone someone who works here."

Skyler didn't seem fazed by Krista's protests. "You were in a premier seating area. Seats like that are hard to come by. How did you get tickets to such an area if you've just arrived in town?"

"Opa's friend Erwin gave them to us. He has season tickets." Krista hated that she sounded defensive when she was telling the truth. "We did nothing wrong."

Skyler offered Krista an apologetic look. "You

aren't the only person we'll talk to. There's a long list of people with access to this place who we'll thoroughly investigate. I'd appreciate your patience as it will take time to work the list to rule out any connection to you."

Translated, Krista was a suspect and would be one for some time. If they dug deep enough into her assumed identity, they'd eventually discover her real name and her supposed role in Toby's death. Then her life would dissolve in chaos again. People would hurl the title murderer at her again. Add bomber to it. Taunt and embarrass her and Opa. Her throat closed with the thought, and she chugged her water under Darcie's watchful eyes.

"You can certainly rule out my Timbers as suspects," Opa announced, taking the attention from her. "None of the players would ever be involved in such a thing."

Krista had to smile at the staunch support of his team.

"Sorry, Otto." Jake grinned. "We'll even have to check into the players.

Opa crossed his arms. "A waste of time, if you ask me. As it is a waste of time checking up on Krista and me, but I will give you Erwin's information so you can contact him to confirm our story."

Determined not to let this team railroad her the way the other cops had, Krista fired a confident look at Skyler. "Do you honestly think I'd bring my grandfather along if I planned to bomb the stadium?"

Brady's brows rose toward thick blond hair. "You could have brought him along for cover. Then something went wrong. You couldn't get out in time and went running to Cash."

Archer faced her. "If you're involved in this, Ms. Curry, it'll go easier on you if you tell us now."

"No…I…" At the wall of stares from the team, the water she'd consumed turned to acid in her stomach. She closed her mouth and looked to Cash for his help.

His eyes that had been so warm and friendly, so interested earlier, were now filled with steely resolve.

Fine. Be that way.

She should've expected his lack of help. She'd trusted him to be on her side once, to rescue Opa, and he'd let her down by tending to the bomb first.

Even if the squad members seemed kind and compassionate at first, they were cops doing their jobs. Cops who didn't trust anyone. She cringed at the thought of the past interrogations. The questions fired at her. Badgering her. Accusing her. Slandering her in the press until no one believed in her innocence, even when they couldn't prove a thing against her.

No. She couldn't trust people like that. A man like that. Even if the bomber showed up on her doorstep to stop her from identifying him, she couldn't count on anyone else. She had to be prepared to protect herself and Opa from the monster willing to kill innocent people.

FIVE

Cash didn't know what to think. Could he believe Krista's story? He looked out the window at her. She sat next to Otto just outside the restaurant, perching on the edge of the bench as if she wanted to bolt. Otto leaned back and crossed his ankles, giving Cash a good look at surprising lime-green sneakers. Cash could see the older guy was tired and wished Skyler would let the pair go home. But she insisted they stay in case the team came up with questions during a quick brainstorming session.

"So." Skyler's no-nonsense tone brought Cash's attention back to the group. Her focus traveled around the table. "Give me your thoughts."

Archer sat forward. "Though this is a real stereotype, being Caucasian makes the bomber less likely to be a terrorist."

Skyler nodded. "But terrorists can be Caucasian, too. Especially ecoterrorists in a green state like Oregon. Still, they rarely resort to bombing, and I can't see an environmental reason for bombing the stadium."

Jake shifted on the edge of the table, a frown drawing down his face. "If he *is* a terrorist, he'll take credit for his work in the next twenty-four hours or so."

"Can't you just look up who bought the ticket for the suspect's seat number?" Darcie asked. "Wouldn't you then have his identity?"

Jake shook his head. "Someone who plants a bomb won't buy a ticket under his real name."

"Plus, the heavy rain kept people away, leaving tons of empty seats in the covered area," Cash added. "The bomber might have simply taken advantage of an empty seat."

"What about the bomb itself?" Skyler asked. "Does it give you any thoughts on who we might be looking for?"

Cash nodded. "The bomb was rudimentary, but it did have an antiremoval device, so that speaks to some experience with explosives. Also, he used blocks of Semtex, which aren't easy to come by." Cash shifted on his feet. "The question I think we need to be asking is, what did he hope to accomplish with the bomb? The backpack was placed by the stanchion holding up the roof. Maybe he wanted to take it down, but without tamping the bomb, it wouldn't likely happen."

"Tamping?" Darcie asked.

"In layman's terms it means aiming the force of the blast in the direction you want it to go to make the explosion more effective."

"Which tells us what exactly?" Jake asked.

"Either he's not very knowledgeable about bombs, or his intent was simply to kill someone in the seating area rather than damage the stadium. Of course, if he had a specific target, then he might've thought to add shrapnel to inflict the most damage, but he didn't."

Brady looked up from a small piece of wood and a knife in his hands. A hyper guy, he often whittled to keep calm. "Setting a bomb is a pretty drastic action just to kill one or two people. I can think of many less risky ways to kill someone."

Jake faced Skyler. "I'm assuming you'll look at security videos and request street cam, business and MAX footage. Not just for today but earlier on."

She nodded. "Though I'd rather not involve the media in this, I'll also have them issue a plea to the public for any pictures or videos taken of the targeted seating section for our review. And we'll get a team on interviewing ticket holders." She grabbed her pen. "What about potential suspects?"

"The obvious one is a stadium employee," Archer said, his intense focus on Skyler. "And event crews or even concessions company staff. They'd have access and if they were unhappy with their work they'd have a motive, too."

"Same with delivery people," Jake tossed out.

"Or recycling company employees who pick up green products."

Skyler's pen raced across the paper.

Cash grinned. "And despite what Otto may think, we also can't rule out the players and coaches. Though I suspect Otto wouldn't mind if we limited our inquiries to the opposing team."

Brady cleared his throat and all eyes turned to him. "Don't forget to add Ms. Curry and Otto."

"Are you honestly liking them for this?" Cash asked. "I mean, we have no motive for her wanting to do this."

Brady met Cash's gaze. "You haven't been in law enforcement all that long, but we all know—"

"The person who reports the crime—" Skyler finished writing and looked up "—is always a suspect until we can prove otherwise. And that includes finding the motive you're speaking of."

"I'm not sure this counts on the motive thing," Darcie said, "but Krista's wearing designer clothes. Not something she could afford on a preschool teacher's salary. And I didn't see a wedding ring so there's not likely a spouse to pay for the clothes."

"She still could be married," Archer said.

The thought left Cash more unsettled than he wanted to think about.

"Or divorced. Or widowed," Jake added.

"Easy enough to find out. I'll ask." Skyler

stepped outside. Cash saw Krista's shoulders go up in a defensive posture at the question.

Was she hiding an involvement in the bombing, or did she simply hate personal questions?

Skyler returned. "Widowed. Four years ago."

Cash sighed, drawing Jake's attention so Cash quickly moved on. "If we're looking at Krista for this, then we should also look into the woman who incited the crowd. I can check a stadium diagram for her seat number. It may not lead anywhere if she was dodging the rain, but it's worth a shot."

"Once you locate the number, I'll make it a priority to find her." Skyler looked around the group. "Any other suggestions or ideas?"

No one spoke.

"Okay, then." Skyler tucked her notebook in her backpack. "As Jake said, I'll be teaming up with the city. We'll both assign considerable resources to the investigation, but with the number of people to be interviewed, it would be great if everyone volunteered time to help."

"I'm game." Brady hopped to his feet.

The others added their agreement.

"Great," Skyler said. "If you'll email your schedules to me, I'll work you in the rotation. And thanks for the help."

"That all?" Brady was clearly itching to get moving. Cash was surprised it had taken him this long to ask.

Jake nodded. "We're good to go."

Brady shot for the door.

"I'll go tell Krista and Otto they're free to leave." Cash headed outside before anyone tried to stop him, especially Skyler, who was coming his way. He stepped into the cold, damp air and zipped his jacket as he approached the pair.

The scent of popcorn lingering in the air spoke of fun and enjoyment, contradicting Otto's fatigued expression. He looked plumb worn-out and still had a long train ride.

Cash met Otto's gaze. "You two look like you could use a ride home instead of taking MAX."

"No," Krista said.

"That is most generous," Otto said at the same time.

She frowned at him. "It's not necessary, Deputy Dixon."

"It's Cash," he said, not liking the formality of her tone for reasons he chose not to analyze. "Necessary or not, I want to help."

"Thank you." Otto smiled. "We will be glad to accept your offer. Might I use the restroom before we go?"

Cash ignored Krista's stare and nodded. "There's one in the restaurant."

"I'll go with you." Krista helped Otto rise and move back into the restaurant.

Skyler eyed the pair as they strolled by. After the door closed, she joined Cash. "What's going on?"

"With what?" he asked, feigning ignorance.

"You and Ms. Curry know each other?"

"No."

"But you find her attractive."

"What red-blooded male wouldn't?" He held up a hand to stop Skyler from continuing. "Don't worry. I don't plan to do anything about it."

"Please don't be offended that I asked about this." She took a step closer. "You haven't been a deputy all that long, and I want to make sure you understand your role here."

He smiled. "You mean other than the red-blooded-male thing?"

She frowned at him. "I'm serious here, Cash."

So was he. He wasn't uncomfortable disagreeing with others on the team. That was the norm for him, but he *was* uncomfortable with his reason for disagreeing today. He couldn't clear Krista from suspicion just because she was pretty and kind to her grandfather. He needed to take a step back. To focus on the evidence in front of him as he'd been taught. To remember Brady spoke the truth—suspect the person who reported the crime until they were ruled out.

He leaned against the wall and let the night play in his memory. He saw Krista running toward him, gripping his arm, her terrified eyes looking up at Otto. "Krista's shock and fear at the discovery of the bomb were real. I'd stake my life on that, and I find it hard to believe she had any part in this."

"Don't make a rookie mistake," Skyler warned. "There are all kinds of reasons she could be involved and still be legitimately terrified."

"Name one," he challenged.

"She could've been working with a partner who stashed the backpack in the stadium earlier and it was her job to retrieve and place the bomb."

"Otto didn't mention seeing her with a backpack and you have to agree he reads like a straight shooter."

"I agree about Otto, but with his obsession with the game it's not hard to believe that he wouldn't notice Krista leaving her seat to retrieve the bomb."

"Okay, say I buy that—which I don't—why would she bring Otto with her if she was going to plant a bomb?"

"He makes great cover for something like this."

"Still, I don't see her risking his life."

"Maybe she didn't think he was at risk. Her partner could have told her there would be more time for her to get out of the stadium, but when she saw the countdown on the cell phone, she realized she couldn't get Otto out in time."

"Maybe." Cash let the idea roll around in his head.

"Or maybe the partner said he only intended to damage the building and the bomb wouldn't go off until after everyone left for the night. Or he might not have told her about the cell phone and only mentioned a timer. When she realized he could call to detonate the bomb at any time, she knew she couldn't get Otto out of there in time, panicked and ran for your help."

"All possible, I suppose."

"But you don't buy any of them."

He shrugged.

"Fine." She sounded irritated, an unusual stance for Skyler. She was their peacemaker. The one who brought people together on their team. But tonight he was seeing a different side of her. The tough investigator. "We can disagree on this as long as we're clear that Ms. Curry is a suspect."

"We're clear." He saw Krista and Opa returning, both of them slipping into their raincoats. Cash pushed off the wall. "I promise to give them a ride, then come running home like a good little boy."

"Right, joke about this as you always do but remember this conversation." Shaking her head, Skyler turned to Krista and handed her a business card. "If you think of anything else that might help, give me a call."

Cash escorted the pair down a ramp to ground level, where he nodded at the officer guarding the exit. Outside, the rain had let up and wispy fingers of steam rose up from the asphalt, disappearing into the dark night. Police cars, both county and city, sat in the lot. Red lights twisted into a swirly cotton candy of fog. A perimeter had been set up and officers dressed in rain gear stood sentry, holding the public at bay.

Cash peered at Otto. "Employees park in an auxiliary lot. It's a bit of a hike. You up for that, or do you want to wait here while I get the car?"

Krista stared across the lot, her expression dark and unreadable. "Maybe we should wait here. We should be fine with all the cops around."

"Stop fussing, Liebchen." A stubborn look claimed the old man's face. "I am able to walk."

Cash didn't want to offend Otto, so he started walking at what he hoped was a slow enough stride to be comfortable. They neared police barricades holding back media crews fairly salivating to one-up each other in their coverage. Paul Parsons from the local News Channel Four TV station was making his way to the front of the crowd. He wore a damp white shirt, and his nondescript brown hair was plastered against his head.

Cash stifled a groan. He'd expected reporters, but he'd rather not face the overly zealous Parsons. He'd tried the patience of FRS team members recently when he'd hounded Skyler after someone tried to kill her. Parsons had made it clear in his reports that he could do a better job in the investigation than the sheriff's department or even better than Skyler's FBI agent fiancé.

But worse, in Cash's opinion, was the way the man had harassed Skyler when she was injured and fragile. Parsons was a bully, plain and simple.

If he started hassling Krista or Opa, Cash would have a hard time not pushing back.

As expected, Parsons slipped past an officer and rushed toward them, his cameraman in tow. Cash put his head down and continued moving.

Krista quickly flipped up her hood, seeming to shrink into her coat. "Do you think he knows who we are? That I saw the bomber?"

"Doubtful, but if he *has* somehow learned you're a witness, just say no comment and keep moving." Cash used his body to shield Krista and Otto while easing them past the tenacious reporter.

Parsons swiveled, planted his feet in front of Krista and shoved the microphone in her face, forcing her to stop. "Is it true, Ms. Curry, that you saw the bomber well enough to give the police a detailed description?"

She took a step back and glanced at Cash. Panic flared in her eyes. An overwhelming protective urge welled up inside Cash—a familiar feeling but not one he'd expected for a woman he barely knew. One who was a suspect in the bombing. It caught him by surprise and made him hesitate. Just a fraction, but long enough for Parsons to seize the moment and step closer.

"Did you see the bomber, Ms. Curry?" he demanded.

Krista jerked back.

Cash did the first thing he could think of. He

grabbed Opa's arm. "I'm sorry, but Ms. Curry's grandfather's had a very trying night, and he isn't feeling well. We need to get him home."

"Yes," Krista mumbled. "He has to get home."

"I won't keep you," Parsons said. "All I want is a simple yes or no. Did you see the bomber?"

"Oh." Opa wobbled and his legs seemed to turn to rubber. He reached for Krista's arm. She clutched his elbow, steadying him.

Cash glanced at the older man, and he winked at Cash.

Nice. The crafty old guy was simply putting on a show for the reporter to distract him from Krista.

"As you can see," Cash said pointedly, "we really need to be going. Unless, of course, you want to be responsible for an elderly man collapsing on your news program."

"Of course not." Parsons knew when to step down and back away.

Cash continued to hold Otto's elbow and hurried ahead. Otto kept up with Cash, but they nearly had to drag Krista. Despite her unspoken desire to get away from the crowd, she kept shooting looks around the area, slowing them down.

Hoping to see what she was searching for, Cash followed her gaze. He saw nothing out of the ordinary. Maybe she feared the bomber was in the crowd of looky-loos that circled the perimeter.

Cash figured the guy was long gone. Unless,

of course, he'd heard the news stories by now and knew Krista's heroic actions had kept the bomb from detonating. If so, he would want to stop her before she had a chance to ID him. Which meant he could have come back and was out in the crowd. Watching. Waiting. Planning to follow them and take Krista out when she was away from the heavy police presence.

Cash was suddenly thankful he'd offered to escort her home. A woman with a sick, elderly man would be a sitting duck for a bomber and without Cash's help, the consequences could be deadly.

SIX

Feeling Cash's focus on her from the car, Krista helped Opa climb the steps to his house. She was torn between wanting Cash gone and wanting him to stay exactly where he was, watching them and making sure no harm came their way. On the ride home, she couldn't stop thinking about what the bomber would do if he knew she could identify him. It would only take one news story to alert him and make him determined to silence her.

The thought made every shadow in the secluded property seem ominous, sending a shiver over her body. She glanced at Cash, wondering if she should ask for his continued help to keep them safe.

"Cash seems like a nice young man," Opa said, oblivious to her concerns.

"He's a cop," she replied as she fitted the key into the lock, reminding herself why Cash was the last person she should trust.

"Not all police officers are bad, Liebchen. If you would stop worrying about the past catching up with you, you would see this young man's positive qualities as I do."

Inside the foyer, she spun in disbelief. "You want to go through all that again? To have people and reporters camping out on the doorstep of your new house? Never getting any peace? Dealing with break-ins and people destroying the place?"

"No, of course not." He stepped inside. "But I doubt that will happen as a result of trusting Cash."

"No." She closed the door, secured the locks, then double-checked them. "It'll happen when a reporter like Paul Parsons wants to find out all he can about me and the FRS team members, including Cash, leak what they know. That'll lead to Parsons eventually discovering my real name is Krista Alger, linking me to Toby's murder and Dad's multitude of crimes."

"You had nothing to do with your father's crimes and Toby's death. Or with scamming those people and the missing money, for that matter. That was all on Toby."

"You and I are the only ones who believe that." Memories of Toby's investment scam that bilked seniors out of their savings came flooding back. No one would accept that she hadn't known about the scam—or about the half-million dollars he'd held in their bank account, then electronically transferred to another account two days before he died. The police never located the money, nor did they locate the person who made the transfer.

Didn't matter. Toby was dead. She was alive and a very convenient suspect, complete with a colorful family background that made her look even guiltier. "I proved that I wasn't home when our wireless network was used to move the money, but the detectives couldn't look beyond Dad's crimes to see me for who I am. All they could say was the apple didn't fall far from the tree."

"But there was no proof, Liebchen. They never charged you with the crime."

"But they wanted to, didn't they? Leaking to the press that I was a person of interest. Making me seem guilty. Hoping I couldn't live under the press's extreme spotlight and would confess."

"There was nothing to confess. If your true name comes out, then Cash will see this and understand."

"I wish, but wishing doesn't change anything." She took Opa's arm. "There's no point in worrying about it now. You've had a long day. Let's get you to bed."

"I am not a baby. I will get myself to bed." He shrugged free of her hold. "Think about what I said about Cash. I think he is an honorable man. If for some reason Skyler keeps you on her suspect list, Cash can be of help."

She stared into the distance. Could she let go

of her terrible experience with the police and believe Cash was the man Opa thought him to be?

"I see the doubt in your eyes, Granddaughter, but trust me in this. I am rarely wrong about people." He shuffled down the hallway before Krista could remind him how wrong he'd been about Toby. She wished Opa had never introduced them.

There she was wishing again. Didn't solve a thing.

She went to her room to change her damp jeans, then settled on the sofa. She turned on the news and waited for the clip of Parsons shoving a microphone in her face. Not surprisingly, the bomb was top news, and Parsons's segment soon came on.

Standing outside the stadium, his update included revealing her name and claiming eyewitnesses believed she was the person who foiled the bomb attempt. He added that they also believed she was the only one who had gotten a good look at the bomber and could identify him. Just as she feared. If the bomber hadn't already figured out that she was the person who stood between him and a long prison term, he would know it now.

She took a deep breath to wait for the footage of her and Opa in the parking lot, but Parsons ended the segment by saying he was working to confirm her role in foiling the bombing, then they moved to another reporter inside the stadium. When the broadcast signed off and the footage hadn't aired, she let out a relieved breath and switched off the TV.

Without her face plastered on the news, she was safe from anyone recognizing her. For now anyway. But Parsons seemed committed to following up, and she wouldn't count on them not using his video in another segment.

As she got up to go to bed, she heard a noise outside. Like a thump. By the back door leading to the deck. Her imagination shot into overdrive. Could the bomber have found her?

Fear coursing through her body, she raced to the hall closet and lifted the door to the crawl space. She felt around for the tote bag she'd hung from a hook and tugged it out.

Her fingers trembled but she managed to open the long zipper and grab her father's old gun. The metal felt cold and reassuring in her hand. She'd spent hours at a gun range with her father and knew how to handle a gun, but never once did she believe she'd have to use it. Still, the training came back. She flipped off the safety and hurried to the back door.

She switched on the exterior light as her heart thundered in her chest. She held her breath and peeked through the blinds.

A raccoon hopped off a turned-over lawn chair and scurried off the deck. Krista sagged against the wall and pulled in gulps of air. Her heart continued to pound, and suddenly, she was back four years ago to a different house she'd shared with Opa after Toby died. To the neighbors who thought she was a murderer. Protesting outside. Breaking in and spray-painting horrible messages on the walls. Trashing the house. Threatening more attacks if she didn't move out of their neighborhood.

It could all happen again. Easily. Quickly, if Parsons dug deep enough and discovered her real identity. She didn't know if she could survive targeted attacks like that again, but when she'd decided to move back from Georgia to take care of Opa, she'd known it was a possibility. Known she might someday have to take off again, though she hated the thought of leaving Opa behind when he was still so ill.

Even so, she'd prepared. Hopefully, she'd thought of everything.

She returned to the hallway and knelt by her bag. It contained clothes, money and extra ammo. Most important, it included a passport, driver's license and credit cards she'd gotten from her father's old friend who issued fake IDs.

She sat back, sighing. How had her life come to this? Contacting a forger. Obtaining yet one more false identity. She felt dirty and underhanded. It was bad enough that she'd gone back to using Curry as her last name. It was the name her father had once procured for her when he was on the run. After she'd left that life behind, she'd left the name behind, too, but going back to it had been her only option after Toby died. The police had frozen all their assets. She had no money. She couldn't even use a credit card, which meant she couldn't escape from the irate neighbors.

She'd felt helpless. Out of control. She'd never let something like that happen again. And she especially wouldn't let Opa go through such a hateful experience again. Nor would she let this bomber get to Opa because of her.

Opa. The one person she loved and trusted. She'd lay down her life to protect him.

She returned the bag minus the gun to her hidey-hole, secured the door, then headed for the sofa in the family room. The loaded gun on her lap, she settled back for a long night of watching.

If the bomber showed up, she'd be ready to stand her ground. To protect herself and her grandfather. No matter the cost.

Cash paced the floor in his condo located on the upper level of an old converted firehouse where the entire team lived. He should be sleeping, but every time he closed his eyes, he saw Krista's last look before she entered her house.

Gone was the evasiveness. Gone was the determination. Instead, fear-darkened eyes that got to him in a way he couldn't explain peered at him. She was worried about the bomber finding her. Or maybe worried about whatever she was hiding.

So what should he do about it, if anything? He'd done his part. Made sure she and Otto arrived home safely. The bomber likely didn't know her identity unless Parsons's segment had aired and her name had been revealed. Then she could be in serious trouble.

Cash couldn't sleep without knowing. He grabbed his laptop and navigated to the station's website, where he found the video from tonight's broadcast. He started Parsons's story playing and sat back to watch. The camera panned the stadium as the relentless reporter announced Krista's full name.

Great. Just as Cash suspected. The bomber could easily know her identity. Question was, could he find her address from that piece of information alone?

Cash assumed the house was in Otto's name. His fingers flew over the keyboard and a quick search of property records confirmed his assumption. Still, the bomber couldn't access databases restricted to law enforcement and retrieve the information as fast as Cash. The bomber would only have the internet at his disposal. So what exactly would he find?

Cash plugged Krista Curry into a search engine. After an hour of searching, only one link led to her, showing she'd worked in a home childcare center in Kennesaw, Georgia.

Odd. In today's social media world, he should

have located far more information about her. She'd obviously worked hard to keep her private life private. Maybe because of whatever she seemed to be hiding.

Cash might want to know her secret, but her caution meant he didn't need to worry if the media or the bomber could easily find her.

A shadowy image of the man she'd described, hunkering down in the thick bushes outside her secluded home, flashed into his mind. Cash had been cautious on the way to Otto's house, but he couldn't guarantee the bomber hadn't tailed them. That the creep wasn't outside their home right now. Krista and Opa alone.

Unprotected.

"Not on my watch," he said and retrieved his gun from the safe. He locked his condo and took the stairs leading to the first-floor common area. A light burning in the shared kitchen had him hesitating. He didn't feel like talking to anyone.

He loved living here, but privacy? Unheard of in the firehouse. Still, he was thankful for the free living quarters. A woman grateful to Darcie for saving her life had donated the place to the county for the FRS members. They each had a private condo on the second and third floors. The first floor was a communal space with a kitchen and dining, family and game rooms.

Trouble was, with their crazy shifts, someone was almost always up. He should have thought of that, as he doubted whoever was awake would support his plan.

He started back up the steps to take the back exit.

"Hey, man." Brady's voice came from the first floor. He wore a freshly pressed county uniform, indicating he was heading out for a patrol shift. "Thought I heard someone out here. You headed out?"

Cash couldn't very well turn back now. He jogged down the steel stairs.

Holding a thick sandwich, Brady leaned against a metal post and crossed his ankles. "Where're you off to?"

Cash considered evading the question or outright lying, but he didn't abide lying. He wouldn't start now. "Thought I'd check on Krista and Otto."

Brady's eyebrow went up, but he didn't say anything, just swung his foot and watched.

"I know what you're thinking," Cash said.

Brady smirked. "You do, do you?"

"It's written all over your face. You think I'm going over there because I've got a thing for Krista."

"Aren't you?" Brady chomped a bite from his sandwich.

"I'm going because Parsons mentioned her name in his broadcast and the bomber might have located her."

"And that's your only motivation?"

Cash thought to deny that his motivations were mixed, but why bother? He and Brady might be able to keep stuff from the others, but with their military backgrounds, they often thought alike and couldn't successfully hide things from each other.

Cash shrugged. "I don't know how to separate the two, I guess."

Brady frowned. "You better figure it out, man, and stay away from her if it's just an attraction thing, or Skyler will have your head on a platter."

Cash respected Skyler—they were good friends—and he would never do anything to interfere in her investigation, unless lives were on the line. That was true of all of his teammates, and Brady needed to recognize that. "So you're saying if a woman you found attractive could be in danger, you'd climb into bed, sleep soundly and forget all about her?"

"You know none of us would do that with anyone—attractive or not. Not if we had some proof that they were in danger. You have proof?"

Cash shook his head.

Brady made strong eye contact. "Ever consider this thing has more to do with losing your team than with anything else? You know…thinking it's up to you to stop anything else bad from happening to the people around you?"

"Maybe," Cash said, avoiding a more detailed answer.

"Hey, I get it." Brady clapped a hand on Cash's

shoulder. "You can't stand the thought that someone else could die on your watch. But you can't extend that watch to everyone you come in contact with. You'll burn out and won't be good to anyone."

"I know that."

"But?"

"Krista and Otto are different somehow. And before you say it's because I've got a thing for Krista, it's not that."

"Then what?"

Cash shrugged.

Brady eyed him. "Like I said, figure it out, or you could burn out and that won't help Krista." Brady turned and strode back to the kitchen.

Cash shrugged into his jacket and went to his car. He tried to concentrate on driving but couldn't get Brady's words out of his head. Brady was right. After losing his team, Cash hated the thought of anyone getting hurt on his watch. He'd done the right thing in requesting the bomb strike in Afghanistan. They'd come under fire, were pinned down, and a strike offered the best chance of saving lives. Cash couldn't have predicted the stupid thing would go astray and he'd be the only team member to survive.

Leaving him to wonder why he'd made it. To question God for eighteen months and not receive a clear answer. Cash usually didn't dwell on things he couldn't change, but he just couldn't shake this. Staying busy was the only way to keep the questions out of his head.

He cranked up the radio. Old favorites on a country station blared through the car until he arrived at Otto's house. Cutting off the headlights, he coasted to a stop well out of view of the rustic place.

Dark and quiet inside, a dim light flashed, then quickly cut off. Suspicious? Maybe. It could be a night-light of some sort, but he wouldn't take any chances.

He tugged his collar up against the cold April wind and strode down the driveway toward the A-frame home, a light drizzle dampening his face. The moon, only a sliver tonight, hid behind dense cloud cover.

He swept his flashlight over the shrubbery abutting the front porch. All clear. He turned the corner heading for the back side overlooking the river swollen from heavy spring rains.

All was quiet. Serene, even.

He'd let his fears make him overreact. Nothing new there. Status quo since he'd left Delta. He turned to go.

A hair-raising scream pierced the air, echoing through the trees.

His blood ran cold.

A second scream split the quiet. Both cries came from inside. A woman.

It was Krista! She was in danger.

Serious danger.

SEVEN

Krista fought hard. Her fists. Her elbows. Punching. Pummeling. Striking anywhere she could. She connected, catching the masked intruder by surprise and shoving him away. Scrambling, she dropped to the floor. Shadows clung to the wood. She groped around. Frantic, hurried movements, searching for her gun. Finally, she touched the edge of the cool metal.

Yes! Only an inch more.

A hand came around her ponytail. Jerked hard. Pain screamed through her scalp. He kept pulling, bringing her to her feet. His arm snaked around her waist. He dragged her toward the door as if planning to abduct her.

She couldn't let that happen. Self-defense courses her father had insisted she take came rushing back. She threw herself back, hit him hard and unsettled him. He flailed around, trying to regain his balance.

She dived for the gun.

"Krista, are you all right?" a male called from outside the back door.

Cash Dixon?

"Cash, is that you?" she yelled, her mind racing to figure out her next steps.

Her attacker paused to listen for a minute. A perfect opportunity to act. She grabbed the gun and scrambled to her feet in front of the door. Lifted the weapon. Aimed.

The intruder held his hands up and inched backward.

"Stop," she screamed, but even she could hear the uncertainty in her voice.

He kept moving.

She raised the gun higher. He suddenly turned and bolted down the hallway toward the back door. She held the gun at the ready but couldn't shoot. Didn't know if she could ever shoot another person. She stepped into the hallway. A wave of light swept in from the open door leading to the deck. She could see a man with a flashlight standing just outside.

Dear God, please let it be Cash.

Her attacker barreled ahead, plowing Cash to the ground. The light went out.

Terrified to act, Krista waited—the gun still in her hand.

"Krista, it's Cash Dixon." The worried voice came from the deck. "Are you all right?"

"I am now," she managed to say.

"Stay there," Cash called out. "I'm going after the intruder."

Relief flooded through her, and she collapsed. The gun's heavy weight pulled her trembling hand to the floor.

The gun. No! She couldn't let Cash see the gun. She doubted her father had gotten it legally. If Cash caught her with it, he'd assume the worst.

"Liebchen," Opa's sleepy voice rumbled down the hallway. "What is all the noise?"

"Everything's okay," she called out as she tucked the gun in her waistband and covered it with her shirt. Despite her shaking knees, she counseled herself to act calm as she went to meet him. In his condition, worrying about her was the last thing he needed.

He rubbed his eyes and blinked. "What is going on?"

"A man broke into the house. I fell asleep on the couch but a noise woke me up." She nodded in the direction of the back door. "Cash Dixon showed up and scared him off. He's still out there, trying to chase the man down."

Concern tightened Opa's eyes. "The bomber?"

"I don't see who else it would be."

"Krista." Cash's voice came from outside.

"Be right there," she shouted, then turned to Opa. "Would you go meet him? I want to splash some water on my face."

"Of course." Opa squeezed her arm. "But then you will let Cash help us. He is a good man."

"You thought Toby was a good man, too, Opa."

Despite her love for him, she couldn't temper her tone. "He might have been a respected member of your church, but that didn't mean he wasn't a liar and a thief."

Opa grimaced. "You are upset so I will ignore your hurtful tone and suggest you pray about this. God will reveal what to do."

"Like he did with Toby?"

"You did not give Him a chance then. You gave up too soon."

She sighed. "I love you, Opa, and I respect you and your opinions, but this is one area we'll have to disagree on." Thankful she'd tucked the gun in the back of her jeans, she gave him a quick hug, then released him before he felt her trembling. "Go talk to Cash. I'll be right out."

She didn't give Opa a chance to argue, but slipped into her bedroom, closing the door behind her. The reality of her attack settled in. She couldn't breathe. Couldn't move. She sank to the floor. Panic threatened to take her over the edge.

No. Focus on the fact that you survived.

But what if Cash hadn't arrived in time? *Stop.* She couldn't dwell on that. She had to find the strength to hold it together for Opa. The man she'd just verbally attacked in the hallway. The man she would never want to hurt. She had to apologize to him. Not yet. Not while she was still this upset.

She sat for uncounted minutes, crying and waiting until the trembling subsided. She crawled to the bed, slid her gun underneath, then pulled herself up by the thick post. In the bathroom, she splashed water over her face, willing her tears to stop before her eyes became swollen and red. She ran a comb through her hair, her scalp tender from the attack. After a few deep cleansing breaths, she stepped into the hallway.

The aroma of fresh coffee greeted her. She found Cash and Opa sitting at the small table in the kitchen. Opa poured his favorite blend of rich, dark coffee from a popular German company. Cash had hung his jacket on his chair as if he intended to stay for some time. He wore jeans, scuffed cowboy boots and a tan waffle-weave shirt that brought out his dark hair. The casual attire should make him look less threatening, but he seemed even more deadly intense. The weapon holstered at his side added to the look. He took a sip of his coffee and grimaced before grabbing the cream.

"Not to your liking?" Opa's eyes twinkled.

Cash cleared his throat. "In my home state of Texas, they'd think it was the thick sludge from oil wells."

"But it is good, no?" Opa replied.

"It takes some getting used to." Krista stepped into the room. "But after a while, you wonder how you could have enjoyed anything else."

Cash set the cup down and ran his gaze over her. "You aren't hurt?"

"No." Her legs still shaky, she sat across from him. "When you called out, the guy ran."

"Any idea who it was?"

She shook her head and took the cup Opa offered. "I was sleeping on the couch when a noise woke me up and I saw him looking in the coat closet. I tried to stop him, but—"

"You tried to stop him," Cash's words shot out. "Why in blazes would you do that?"

She sat back from his harsh tone.

"Sorry, I didn't mean to yell at you, but come on, Krista. The guy could've hurt you. You should have run out the door while you had the chance."

She didn't like his bossiness, but she had to admit she liked hearing her name tumble off his lips. Despite his frustration, it came out honey warm and smooth in his Southern drawl.

Focus. "I wouldn't leave Opa behind."

Opa smiled at her. "As I wouldn't leave you, Liebchen."

Cash wrapped long fingers around his mug, gripping it tight enough to turn his fingers white. "So what happened next?"

"We fought," she said vaguely so she wouldn't have to mention her gun. "He dragged me to the front door like he planned to abduct me. You arrived, and he ran off."

Cash ground his teeth for a moment. "You're sure you didn't recognize this man?"

"He was the right size for the bomber, but it was dark and he wore a ski mask so…" She shrugged.

"I caught a quick look at him as he fled and agree that he fits your description of the bomber." Cash paused and took a sip of the coffee. He looked as if he wanted to grimace but held it back.

"It is okay if you do not like the coffee, Cash." Opa smiled. "I will not hold it against you."

"Hey." Cash's tone lightened. "I don't give up easily. I'll keep trying it."

Krista was certain his statement held double meaning, but she was too tired to think about it.

"I called Jake," he continued. "An officer's on the way to secure the scene and Skyler will be dispatched, too. Plus, Jake issued an alert for the guy and asked for increased patrols in the area."

Opa settled his hand on Krista's, telling her all was forgiven for her outburst in the hallway. "How likely are they to find this man?"

Cash swung his gaze to Opa. "Honestly, not very likely. The woods are pretty dense along the river, so he could get away without being seen."

Cash's description of their setting highlighted the dangers that country living brought. As much as Krista didn't want them to see how deeply the attack was affecting her, she couldn't control the shiver that worked over her body.

Cash appraised her. "I've been assuming you were attacked by the bomber, but I should ask

if you have reason to think it could be someone else."

"No," she said adamantly. "It has to be him."

"We probably should consider that this could
be a random break-in. I haven't heard of any bur-
glaries in the area, but Skyler will look into it and
call in the forensic team to process the house."

"Would a random burglar try to drag me out
the door?"

"If he was panicked and wasn't thinking clearly,
maybe. But you're right in thinking that would
be odd."

"This bomber," Opa said. "How do you think
he found out where Krista lives?"

"Good question." Cash eyed Krista. "I suspect
he heard her name on the news like I did, then
went to the internet. But before I came over here,
I searched and found nothing. Not even a Facebook account. Maybe he's better at searching than
I am."

Cash had dug into her past. Of course he had.
This was just the beginning, and she doubted he
was the only one looking. The time of her discovery was coming closer.

Her stomach cramped, but she forced her expression to remain neutral. "I'm a very private
person. I doubt anyone will find much." *At least
not using the name Krista Curry.*

"Hey, don't get me wrong. I'm all for privacy. As

a deputy, I see people all too often who have gotten into trouble for sharing things on the internet."

"Fortunately, this house is in my name," Opa said. "But I guess it doesn't matter as somehow the bomber made the connection." He paused and stroked his whiskers. "I suppose he will try this again."

Cash nodded. "It's likely he'll come back."

Krista jerked her head to look at Cash. "You really think so? Even after he was almost caught?"

"It's a strong possibility."

Her heart fell and a terrified, "Oh, no," slipped out of its own accord.

"Don't worry." Cash met her gaze. "I'll be sticking to you like glue until the bomber is brought in and you're safe."

"What? No." She sat forward. "I'm sure that's not necessary."

He studied her for a few minutes before he crossed his arms, the corded muscles straining the fabric of his shirt. "Trust me. It's very necessary. We have a guy running around who wasn't afraid to kill countless people in the stadium. You think he'd hesitate to kill one more person?"

"He is right." Opa locked gazes with Krista. "Not only will you say yes to his help, but you will smile and thank him for it."

Fine. She got it. She needed Cash Dixon's help to stay safe—if not for her own sake, then to protect her grandfather, who would also be at risk if

EIGHT

Yawning, Cash walked Skyler to the door and glanced at his watch on the way. Forensics had taken until 6:00 a.m. to finish processing the scene. Krista had gone to shower for work, and Otto was resting. When Cash took Krista to the preschool, they would drop Otto off at his friend Erwin's house for safety.

Skyler opened the door and turned to look at him. "Since you're off today, you might as well go home and get some sleep. There's nothing you can do here."

"I'll hang out for a bit. Just to make sure our suspect doesn't try to take another crack at Krista."

Skyler stepped onto the porch without a comment. "Call me if anything comes up."

He was risking a lecture on personal involvement and should keep his mouth shut, but he didn't care. "And you'll keep me apprised of any new developments in the investigation?"

She eyed him as he expected but then nodded. "All I'll say for now is watch yourself, Cash, and keep my warning in mind." She let her gaze linger for a moment before jogging down the steps to her car.

Her warning wasn't necessary. Cash had thought of little else since Skyler first suggested that with limited information about Krista on the internet the only way the bomber located her was because he knew her. Cash didn't want to consider that possibility, but it was getting harder to ignore Krista's ongoing evasive behavior. His Special Forces and law enforcement training had taught him to read people, and he suspected she was hiding something. Maybe related to the bombing. Maybe not. Didn't matter. He planned to find out if she was trying to conceal something.

First, he needed to ensure her safety.

He stepped outside to perform a threat assessment before departure. Parsons had aired another story this morning, this time flashing Krista's picture for all to see. With the lack of internet leads on Krista, Cash doubted reporters could find Otto's property this quickly, but Cash wouldn't take a chance.

He circled the home, looking behind frosty shrubbery and under the deck before walking the driveway lined with tall pines. Nearing the road, he spotted a black SUV idling on the shoulder across the road. The driver was in a perfect location to watch Krista, which it seemed as if the occupant had been doing for a while as the windows were fogged from the inside.

Cash's intuition warned him to take care. He slipped into the woods and inched closer for a better look. Even this close, he could only make out the shape of a large male sitting behind the wheel.

Could be a reporter but Cash still doubted the press had found her.

The bomber? Her attacker? Maybe, but if so, why park in plain sight?

Cash wanted to rush the vehicle, but he'd likely scare the guy off. Instead, he moved deeper into the woods until he could make out the license plate.

He called dispatch only to discover the SUV was a rental. Meant it probably wasn't a reporter, but a lost tourist stopping to get his bearings. Could still be her attacker, though.

Cash slipped back through the trees to reassess and saw the guy clear a small circle on the window. He sat there, peering out, staring down Krista's drive, the minutes ticking by.

Cash's instincts fired an alert and he settled his hand on his gun.

"Cash." Krista's voice came from the porch, the area in full view of the driver. "We're ready to go."

Cash's heart dropped, and he jumped onto the driveway.

"Go back inside, Krista," he yelled. "Now!"

Her eyes fearful, she turned and the SUV's powerful engine revved. Cash drew his weapon and spun. The engine roared louder. Cash stood ready, waiting for the car window to open and a gun to appear, but the driver shifted into gear and squealed away, sending gravel flying.

Cash wanted to check on Krista, but he stood his ground until the vehicle was out of sight, then pulled out his phone to request backup.

Maybe he was overreacting, but if this was their bomber and he was brave enough to show up in broad daylight mere hours after he'd assaulted Krista, the creep was willing to go to extreme measures to achieve his goal. And what could that goal be other than eliminating the only witness who could identify him for his crime?

In the family room, Cash gave Krista a vague description of the car that had just raced off. Krista suspected he'd chosen not to share many details of the incident to keep her from panicking. It didn't work.

This guy, the bomber, was persistent. Breaking into their house. Attacking her. Perhaps killing or abducting her if Cash hadn't arrived on time. And now, he'd come back. Could come back again. Maybe succeed in his mission.

Fear sent her pulse racing. She shot a look around the room, searching for comfort. Her gaze settled on Cash. Cash was here. Standing tall and strong. The man she'd been fighting every step of the way, yet he made sure she and Opa weren't harmed. Even when she'd been so unfriendly to him. She didn't deserve his care.

She gave him a genuine smile. "Thank you for being here with us. Especially after I've been less than cooperative."

"No problem." His tone remained level, but a hint of a smile followed. "It's what I do."

"You can't possibly do this for everyone who needs help."

"No." He met her gaze levelly.

"So why me? Us?"

He shrugged but held her gaze, and she felt a change in him. Not the spark of physical attraction that clearly existed between them. Something softer. Different. Special.

"I can't put my finger on it, but I know you need me, and I'd be a real jerk to leave." His voice was low and husky, his warm accent soothing her unease.

The word *trustworthy* came to mind. He genuinely appeared to be a man of honor. Could she really believe he was everything he seemed to be? Everything Opa believed he was?

What would happen if he discovered Toby's murder and the accusations? Would Cash stay by her side then? She didn't really know enough about him to have a clue how he would react, and she needed to remember that.

She broke the magnetic pull and took a step back. "Well, thank you again for your help."

"I second that." Opa joined them and fired a pointed look at Krista. "I'm glad my Liebchen has finally realized we can use your assistance."

She didn't want to go there again. She stepped toward the front door and dug her keys from her purse. A gum wrapper fell to the floor, giving her an idea.

"I forgot to do something," she said to Cash. "Would you get Opa settled in the car while I take care of it and lock up?"

"I do not need settling," Opa grumbled.

"But you could use a few extra minutes to get down the stairs," Cash commented, surprising Krista that he was on her side.

"That I could." Opa frowned as he started down the stairs. "Getting old is a bear."

Cash grinned at Opa. "But think how wise you are now. Or maybe I'm wrong and you're just a wise guy."

Opa laughed joyfully. Krista was thankful for the care and consideration Cash was showing to her grandfather. She was tempted to think he was doing it to get on her good side, but he genuinely seemed to like Opa. And Opa had made it clear he liked and respected Cash.

At the bottom of the steps, Cash turned and looked up at her. "You'd best get moving, or you'll be late for work."

She went inside for a small piece of paper, then waited until Cash was distracted with Opa before inserting the paper into the doorjamb and closing the door. If anyone entered the house while they were gone, the paper would fall out, alerting her that someone had been inside.

Shaking her head, she locked the door and hurried to the car. She couldn't believe she had reason to use the trick her father had taught her when she was a teen and they'd been on the run from the police. She'd tried to forget those days. The days back when she'd believed in her father's innocence. She especially wanted to forget his lies meant to keep her by his side as he evaded capture for murdering his partner. To keep their lives a secret from everyone—including Opa. Maybe things would have been different if her father was Opa's son instead of his son-in-law. Maybe then her father wouldn't have run, or maybe Opa wouldn't have wanted to report her father to the police.

Maybe, maybe, maybe. Her life was filled with maybes and thinking about it changed nothing.

"Everything okay?" Cash asked.

She nodded and looked out the window before she gave away her unease. Thankfully, he didn't press her. Instead, he focused on checking the mirror, watching for a threat. He didn't let down his guard the entire drive. Even when they stopped at Erwin's house, he insisted on evaluating the home's security and giving the men pointers on how to stay safe.

Krista hugged her grandfather. "We'll pick you up after work. I'll call if anything changes."

He stepped back and his lips tipped in his usual, comforting smile. "Do not worry about me, Liebchen. Just enjoy your day."

Cash took her elbow and directed her down the pathway. He held her close to his side, his touch making her unreasonably happy. Not the warmth of it, but the care he was exhibiting for her, too. He was dedicated, committed, kind and considerate. All the things her father had never been.

All the things she'd thought Toby had been.

The reminder of how wrong she'd been about Toby was like a bucket of cold water on her warm feelings for Cash. She put distance between them, and as she climbed into the car, she cautioned herself yet again to keep up her guard.

Grinning, Cash climbed behind the wheel. "Your grandfather has met his match in Erwin."

She swiveled to face him. "You seem so at ease with Opa. Like maybe you have a great relationship with your own grandfather."

Cash's smile fell. "My family is kind of complicated."

His sudden change in tone sent her suspicions flaring. She should take heed. Back off. But the need to ask about his complicated family—to know more about him as a man—had her rushing ahead. "Complicated how?"

He stared at the road, either ignoring her or searching for the right words.

"It's okay if you don't want to talk about it. Trust me, I understand complicated families."

"It's not that. I just don't know where to start."

"How about with the parts that weren't complicated?"

"Can't remember back that far." A sarcastic laugh slipped out.

"I understand," she said again, but truth be told she was hurt that he wouldn't tell her. She had no right to know anything about him. After all, she didn't plan to talk about her past.

He gripped the wheel, his mouth opening, closing, then opening again before he said, "Things changed when my parents were killed in a car accident. I was eight and was shipped off to my grandparents. They were older when they had Mom and weren't prepared to raise another child. And I..."

He shook his head as if the memories were painful. "Man, I was a pain. A huge, royal one. Took out all my grief over losing my parents on Gram and Granddad." He took a long breath and blew it out. "Granddad's a good ole boy from way back. He believes in harsh discipline. It was the wrong way to keep me in line, and I pushed him to the limit. When they reached the end of their rope, I went to live with my other grandparents. Same kind of thing happened. Then I spent time with my uncle. I was a piece of work." He shook his head again. "A real piece. They all decided I'd do better in the foster care system to get counseling none of them could afford."

She heard the pain in his voice. Who wouldn't be hurt if their family passed them off to strangers? She was honestly surprised he'd opened up enough to tell her all of that.

"I get it," she assured him. "At least part of it. My mom died when I was fourteen. I wasn't sent to foster care, but I can relate to the acting-out part." She smiled at him. Maybe to cheer him up. Maybe to thank him for sharing. Maybe because, when she forgot for a moment that she shouldn't trust him, she actually liked being with him. "Did foster care work out for you?"

"Nah. By that time, I'd gotten it into my head that I didn't deserve a family. Got into more trouble. Things escalated until a judge gave me a choice—the military or prison."

"I'm sorry, Cash," she said sincerely. "That must have been hard."

He shrugged. "Worked out okay. The army set me right. I'm thankful I chose it."

"After how you described yourself, I'd have thought you would have suffocated under army discipline."

"I did at first." He smiled, a big genuine one that said he wasn't at all sad about that experience.

"Ended real fast, though, and I finally found a place I belonged."

"And yet you're no longer in the army."

He clenched his jaw and focused on the road before glancing back at her. "That's a story for another day."

She'd obviously hit another sore spot. One he wasn't willing to discuss. Not that she deserved for him to open up. Not after hiding her own past.

Still, it hurt. Deep inside. Reminded her of the way her father and Toby had treated her. She'd learned a hard lesson from them. When she'd dug deep enough, she found a terrible, earth-shattering secret. She'd had enough of people lying to her to last a lifetime. She wouldn't risk believing in another person, only to have the same consequences take her down again.

NINE

Cash stood outside Krista's classroom. He'd spent the morning dividing his attention between watching for potential threats and enjoying the sight of Krista with her preschoolers. She was animated and joyful, her face lighting up around the children.

He could now understand the point made by the preschool director earlier in the day. Krista had offered to take a leave of absence if her situation would cause a problem for the center. But Peggy said the children would be devastated if Krista suddenly disappeared. Cash knew nothing about children, but apparently, preschoolers needed routine and consistency in their lives and Krista leaving unexpectedly would throw them for a loop. Peggy added, since Cash was a sworn deputy and had obviously cleared a criminal background investigation, having him in the building combined with their already strong security protocol would keep the children safe.

He checked his watch. Near noon and time for Skyler to arrive with the sketch artist. The secured building meant he would have to let Skyler in using an access code. He signaled to Krista that he was leaving. She smiled up from where she and the children sat in a circle. The smile lit her face, a radiance coming from inside that no one could fake. She loved her job and these children. He imagined being the recipient of such affection from a woman and his heart came alive for the first time in aeons.

Shocked at his reaction, he headed outside. Giving in to his emotions when he needed to keep his focus on protecting Krista was the last thing either of them needed.

The drizzle had stopped and clouds had split to let the sun shine through. Skyler stepped from her car to join their sketch artist, Rick, on the walkway. A computer case hung from her shoulder and she held a tray with brown paper bags and drinks.

Cash took the tray. "I hope this's lunch for all of us."

"Yeah, I'll give you the bill later." She winked at him.

"Thanks for thinking of it." He smiled.

"No problem. I didn't want Ms. Curry to miss her lunch."

"She'll be free in a few minutes. I have a room all set up." Cash unlocked the door and led the way to a parent meeting room.

Rick settled in a chair at the far end of a long table and unpacked sketching tools. Skyler removed a sandwich from the bag and set it along with chips and a drink in front of Rick. Thanking her, he went back to his task.

She joined Cash at the other end of the table and handed him a sandwich. He opened it and eyed the thick wheat bread with turkey and mounds of sprouts. His stomach rumbled, but he decided to wait for Krista.

Skyler looked up from the bag. "Everything going okay here?"

"No sign of the intruder or of Krista's early-morning visitor." Cash took a long sip of an icy cold soda.

"I noticed you charmed the director into giving you an access code."

"Actually, I didn't even need to ask. She wants to do everything she can to help Krista." He cast a reproachful look at Skyler. "Besides, I resent the fact that you think I charm women to get what I want."

Skyler sat next to him. "I don't think you do it for selfish reasons or on purpose, for that matter. It's just your good ole boy Southern personality to be charming."

"And that's a bad thing?"

She watched for a long moment. "Not as long as your intentions are clear. Otherwise, the recipient of one of your guaranteed-to-melt-a-heart looks might see you as a player."

"Player? Me?" His voice shot up. "You're traipsing down a road even a hunting dog wouldn't take."

"Am I? It's what I thought when I first met you. That, and you use it to cover up deeper issues."

He was starting to get mad and crossed his arms. "I thought you were here for the sketch, not to use your psychology degree to analyze me."

"I am and you're changing the subject as you always do." Skyler nodded at the window, where they could see Krista coming toward the room. "Maybe we should ask Ms. Curry what she thinks of you."

"What? You're crazy," he nearly shouted. "I am not asking Krista about that."

"Why not?"

"Stop it, Skyler. This is none of your business."

"Ah, now we're getting to the real Cash."

He gave Skyler a warning look. "I have a professional relationship with Krista, nothing more."

"If you say so." She met his stubborn stare with one of her own. "It'd be good for you to remember that, then. You know, instead of looking at her like she's the woman you've been waiting your whole life for."

"Enough." Cash fisted his hands. He liked Skyler, but sometimes she didn't know when to let sleeping dogs lie. Between Darcie as the mom of the group and Skyler dedicated to solving all of their issues, Cash wanted to scream at times. She'd been especially bad since she'd found love and gotten engaged to Logan Hunter. Now she wanted all of them to be as happy. She couldn't seem to understand that a woman in his life right now was not the ticket to his happiness.

Krista entered the room, and Cash quickly introduced Rick before Skyler could say anything about this player business.

"I hope doing this sketch doesn't take your appetite away." Skyler set a sandwich and drink in front of Krista as she took a seat next to Rick.

"Even if it does, I'll still eat. I need every bit of the strength I can muster to work with preschoolers." A lopsided grin followed her words.

"How long have you worked with this age group?" Skyler asked.

Krista's smile faltered. "Just a few years."

Skyler started to ask a follow-up question but Krista rushed on. "We really should get to the sketch so I'm not late for the afternoon session."

"Of course," Skyler said, but Cash saw residual questions linger in her eyes. She'd obviously noticed Krista's evasive behavior, and as Skyler came to sit by Cash at the other end of the table, she kept glancing back at Krista.

"Any new developments in the investigation?" Cash asked, then finally bit into the sandwich and stifled a groan over the tangy goodness of the deli's special sauce.

"We confirmed Krista's story about their tickets." Skyler kept her voice low, likely to keep the information from Krista. Not that she could hear them from where she sat.

"We processed the bomb for fingerprints, but didn't lift any," Skyler continued. "Bomber most likely wore gloves. We also reviewed ticket sales. The woman who sounded the alarm didn't have a ticket for the seat you pointed out, and the bomber's seat belonged to a season ticket holder. He showed me the ticket proving he didn't attend, and he obviously didn't give the ticket to anyone."

"So our bomber is an employee, a vendor or some other staff or team member. Or even a spectator who sat in a section he wasn't ticketed for. Meaning we didn't narrow things down a whole lot."

"Exactly. Once I have a sketch of the bomber, I'll be interviewing spectators to see if they recognize him. If he was targeting a specific person, hopefully we'll find a connection." She sipped her soda. "Oh, and I should mention, there aren't any surveillance cameras at the employee and service entrances to the stadium. So it's not surprising that someone smuggled the bomb in via those routes without anyone seeing."

The disappointing news ended their discussion, and they ate in silence while Rick finished the sketch. Krista gave her final approval and Rick handed his drawing to Skyler, then started packing up his belongings.

Krista dumped her lunch trash. "I need to get back to my classroom. I hope the sketch is helpful."

Skyler studied it. "The detail is excellent. It's exactly what we need."

"Good." Krista looked at Cash, her expression uneasy. "I'll see you later, right?"

"Don't worry." He smiled to lessen her concern. "I'm not going anywhere. I'll be reviewing surveillance video for the stadium entrances with Skyler, but I can see anyone who comes to the door."

"We have outdoor time at two-thirty."

He gave her another reassuring smile. "I won't let you go out to the playground alone."

She looked as if she wanted to say something else but departed.

"I've gotta take off, too." Rick shouldered his case.

"I'll walk you out." Cash escorted Rick to the door and then returned to the meeting room to find Skyler sitting behind her laptop.

Cash sat next to her. "Did you mean it about the quality of the sketch, or were you just being nice?"

"It's good—very detailed." Skyler frowned.

"Why the frown, then?"

"What if my theory is right—that Krista and

the bomber know each other and that's why she can describe him so well?"

"You're still thinking of her as a suspect?"

"Of course. We haven't discovered anything to rule her out. I can't find much about her. Not even a record of a marriage. I'm wondering if she lied about being a widow."

"You check all states?"

She rolled her eyes. "You know I couldn't have contacted more than the likely counties in Oregon and Georgia this fast, but I've got someone on it."

"Maybe she got married in Vegas."

"Maybe."

"Why didn't you ask her about it?"

"I don't want to tip her off in case the death of her alleged husband somehow plays into this." Skyler sounded so skeptical it made Cash mad.

He crossed his arms. "What about a motive to tie her to the bomb? You haven't found that, either. And what about the break-in? She was almost abducted, for crying out loud."

"Doesn't mean she wasn't working with this guy. Maybe he turned on her. Happens all the time in the criminal world."

The thought of Krista as a criminal made Cash sick. "Have you found anything to suggest she has experience with explosives or any connection to the stadium that would allow her to sneak the bomb in?"

"Not yet, but you know better than I do that experience isn't necessary to transport a bomb."

"True," he said and wished he could come up with a better answer.

"As to a motive, we're working down the list of people with stadium access. We could still find that she's connected to someone. And we still might find something that gives her a motive. Which means, we can't take her off our list until we've questioned everyone else or found the bomber." Skyler took a long breath and watched Cash.

He didn't like the way she was staring at him. "Stop giving me that look and tell me what you're thinking."

"I realize Krista's being helpful," Skyler said and Cash waited for the "but" he knew was coming. "But honestly, I get the feeling she's hiding something. I'm not sure it's related to the bomb, but there's something going on with her. Then there's the lack of information we can find about her. With the way everyone shares online these days, that's a red flag."

Cash had thought the same thing last night, but he found himself needing to defend Krista. "She's a private person. Doesn't make her a bomber."

Skyler leaned closer, her gaze pointed and direct. "Look, I get that you don't want it to be Ms. Curry, but we have to remain objective until we can rule her out. Can you do that?"

"I hope so," he said honestly. "I haven't had the kind of experience you've had with investigations, but I've gotten to know Krista and Otto a bit, and I don't get the feeling that she's the type of person to do something like this." Skyler opened her mouth to speak, but Cash held up his hand. "I promise to do my best to keep an open mind, and I'll report anything I notice that can help with the investigation, whether it's in her favor or not. That's the best I can do right now."

"That's good enough for now." Skyler turned to her computer. "Let's get to work reviewing the security files."

Cash shifted his chair to maintain a clear view of the front door, and they compared footage to the sketch for the next few hours. Every thirty minutes, he went to Krista's classroom to check on her. Skyler raised her eyebrows each time, but Cash didn't care. Skyler was tasked with finding the bomber. Cash had tasked himself with protecting Krista.

Despite the frequent breaks, just before Cash had to go out to the playground they found hazy video of two men who fit Krista's description of the suspect and resembled the sketch.

Cash stood. "At least the video produced a few leads."

Skyler started packing up her things. "I'll have the team work on tracking the men down. Hopefully we'll get somewhere with them. And I'll get the sketch out to law enforcement."

"What about the media? Shouldn't you send it to them, too?"

She shook her head. "When the press gets hold of this, they'll dig until they find out the sketch came from Ms. Curry. If she really is innocent, I don't want the bomber to know how well she can describe him and come after her again." Skyler paused and met Cash's gaze, her expression deadly serious. "Suspect or not, I don't want to do anything to increase the danger to Ms. Curry."

For once Cash agreed with Skyler. Krista was in danger. Just how much remained to be seen.

TEN

Krista finished her short break and headed to the playground to resume watching her class. After taking the kids outside, Peggy had stepped in for Krista's afternoon break. She'd needed the time. How she'd needed it. The morning preschool class had been a handful and the afternoon group was unruly, too. They were most likely picking up on her stress, and she had to do a better job of controlling it.

On the playground, she was surprised to find the staff lining the children up at the door. The schedule called for another fifteen minutes of outdoor time, and she needed them to burn off energy.

Concern mounting, Krista immediately took a head count to make sure they were all present, then approached Peggy.

Peggy peered through thick glasses. "I'm glad you're back."

"Is everything okay?"

Peggy lowered her voice. "Cash saw a man pull up and watch the playground. He said it was probably nothing, but suggested we take the children inside." She gestured at the chain-link fence facing the road.

Cash stood on the street side of the fence, motioning for Krista to step closer. His defensive posture left her feeling even more unsettled. "Do you mind if I ask Cash for more details before taking over?"

"Go ahead. We'll get the kids inside."

Krista crossed the playground to Cash. "What's going on?"

"Don't react but casually glance at the vehicle across the street and tell me if you recognize the car."

Trying not to whip her head around, she slowly turned and pretended not to look at the big black SUV parked at the curb. She squinted in the bright sunlight and still couldn't see the occupant from her angle, but she didn't know anyone in Portland with this make of car. "Could be a parent or even someone stopping to take a phone call since it's illegal to talk while driving here."

"No," he said, the concern in his voice apparent in the single word. "It's the same vehicle as the one outside your house this morning."

"Are you sure?"

He nodded. "Same license plate. We have to assume this person is here because of you. Is there any reason someone other than the bomber would be watching you?"

She shook her head, but then her mind traveled to Toby, and she felt sick to her stomach. She'd been focused on the bomber, but what if detectives from Toby's case were in that car? Since Portland had a low homicide rate and little turnover in detectives, she suspected the detectives were still employed and wouldn't forget Toby's unsolved case.

It wasn't a far-fetched idea that they'd want to talk to her again now that she was back in town. It wasn't even a long shot after this morning's news report that they'd recognized her and decided to tail her. Or it could be one of the people Toby scammed. They'd been very vocal about getting back at her for the loss of their money.

And, if it truly was the same car from this morning, Cash could have figured out who owned the vehicle. Maybe this was a test to see if she would tell the truth.

"Krista." Cash rubbed a hand over his jaw. "Did you think of someone?"

She couldn't share her thoughts, but she also couldn't lie. "I haven't interacted with anyone but Opa and his medical team since I've been back. Oh, and Erwin, too. Plus my coworkers and my students' parents, of course." She looked away as guilt over sidestepping his question ate at her.

She felt Cash appraising her, but she refused to look at him.

"Then I guess I'd better go have a talk with the man."

"Be careful." She glanced at him and, for a second, she considered telling him everything. Only for a second. "I'd better get inside to my class."

"I'll let you know what I find." He left her standing there and crossed the road. He was all restrained power and hard muscle as he moved toward the SUV. She wouldn't want to be the person sitting in the car when he caught up to them. He'd reached the middle of the street when the driver gunned the engine and screeched from the curb.

She saw Cash dig out his phone. She suspected he was reporting the car and asking for an ID on the license plate, if he hadn't already asked this morning. If the man in the vehicle was indeed a detective, Cash was about to learn her secret.

With a heavy heart, Krista went inside and threw herself into her work to avoid thinking about the pending discovery. She succeeded well enough to fool the children—and even to fool herself a little. But the minute she opened the door at the end of the day and caught Cash waiting nearby, the worry returned. After the last child departed, Cash joined her at the door. She held her breath, waiting to see what he'd say.

He glanced at his watch. "I'm surprised to see the kids go home this early. I thought you worked until four."

"I do, but that includes an hour for cleanup and prep for tomorrow."

"Anything I can do to help?"

Good. He hadn't mentioned the car. "You could clean and disinfect tables if you wouldn't mind."

"Just tell me what to do."

She grabbed a spray bottle with a weak bleach-and-water mixture along with paper towels and handed them to him. Their fingers brushed, and she felt a warm rush of emotions. Surprised, she stepped back, earning a lift of his eyebrow.

"Spray all the surfaces and let the solution sit for two minutes," she said quickly. "Then dry with the towels."

"Two minutes, huh? Do I have to time it and be that precise?" He grinned at her, his teasing tone giving her hope that he hadn't learned her secret.

She gave a mock serious nod. "To the nano-second."

He laughed, and her heart clutched at the care-free sound. Before she did or said anything she'd regret, she grabbed the list of items needed for tomorrow's lesson plans and started for the door.

On the way to the supply cabinet, she glanced at him. The child-size furnishings always looked small, but they appeared minuscule when he hunkered over the table. She watched the muscles in his forearm ripple as he sprayed and the larger ones in his shoulders roll as he wiped.

He suddenly stood back and caught her watching. She expected another flirtatious smile, but he was solemn. Maybe he'd simply delayed telling her what he'd discovered.

"So the two minutes," he said, looking confused. "Did the person who came up with this actually time it? I mean, do germs still live at a minute fifty-nine seconds or something?"

She let out a breath and shrugged. "My degree's in education, not biology. We follow the health department's guidelines."

"Ah," he frowned. "Someone probably blew hours and hours studying this and wasted tons of tax money funding the study."

"I guess so, but it wasn't a waste of money in my book. I want the children to be in the best and safest environment possible."

"So do I, but honestly…" He shook his head. "I wish some of that money could go to the military to keep soldiers safer."

She heard immeasurable pain in his voice. "Sounds like you saw some action."

He gave her a mock salute. "Delta Force at your service, ma'am. We deployed all over the world but most recently in Afghanistan."

His tone was joking, but there was more that he wasn't saying. It was there in the dejected angle of his head and the sadness of his eyes. She couldn't imagine being at war. Seeing the ugly things he must have seen. With his honorable personality, he surely wanted to correct the injustices he encountered.

And Delta Force, wow! They were an elite group. Highly trained. That was the extent of her military knowledge, and she'd learned that little bit from a video game Toby used to play. She started to comment on the game, then clamped her hand over her mouth. Mentioning Toby would open the door for Cash to ask questions about her marriage. Questions she couldn't answer.

Cash arched a brow. "Don't tell me you're one of those people who don't support the military."

"No," the word shot out. "I respect the men and women who protect us."

"Then what were you going to say?"

"Nothing important."

He watched her intently for a moment before lifting a shoulder in a whatever shrug. "We should get back to work so I can get you and Otto home."

Krista felt let down for some reason. As if Cash thought cleaning the tables was more important than trying to find out what she was hiding. She didn't want him to be interested in her or learn her secret. So why was she disappointed?

Because he'd distracted her from her crazy, out-of-control life, or because talking with him as a woman might do when interested in a man felt normal? Which meant for the briefest of moments she could entertain the thought that she might someday have everything she'd once hoped for with Toby.

A pipe dream.

She had no reason even to think about a man. Any man. Not with her poor judgment and the murder accusation hanging over her head. Not to mention a bomber stalking her.

This attraction to Cash Dixon was crazy. Totally crazy. And pointless—nothing could come of it.

She needed to get away from him.

"Be right back," she said and hurried to get supplies from the hallway cabinet. By the time she'd returned to the classroom, he'd finished all the tables and was perched on the corner of her desk with his phone in his hand.

How wonderful it would be if a man was waiting for her like this. Waiting to take her home. To share a life.

He looked up and smiled at her. Her heart constricted and without thinking, she returned his smile. Their eyes met. Held. The air between them turned electric. He sucked in a breath and blew it out.

That was all she needed to come back down to reality. "Let me set out these supplies and we can go."

She worked quickly to distribute the items to the tables, and they were soon on the road to pick up Opa. They didn't speak on the drive. A good thing, because she wasn't ready to talk about what had transpired between them. The more time she spent with him, the more she was forgetting one of the most valuable lessons she'd learned—trust no one except Opa.

They picked Opa up and, thankfully, he chatted all the way to his house, keeping Cash laughing with stories of his day. Krista usually loved Opa's stories but couldn't join in the laughter today. She watched out the window for the rest of the drive.

Cash parked at the foot of the stairs and climbed out. "If you want to get the front door open, Krista, I'll help Otto up the stairs."

She didn't argue but climbed the steps while digging her key ring from the deep recesses of her purse. Cash soon stepped up beside her and took her keys. For a time she was distracted by watching his hands turn the lock, but then she caught sight of the paper she'd tucked in the doorjamb lying near the railing. She jumped back before realizing such a move would draw Cash's attention.

She turned to her grandfather to avoid Cash's intent gaze. "Did you come home at all today, Opa?"

"No, why?"

Not the answer she'd hoped for. Someone had been here. Today. While they were gone.

Fear iced her heart.

She looked around, searching for how to handle this. She couldn't tell Cash that she knew how to set traps for potential intruders. He'd grill her for details of her past. She also couldn't let them walk into the house unprepared.

"What is wrong, Liebchen?" Opa asked.

Opa was counting on her to make sure he was safe. She had to pick up the paper. "I put paper in the doorjamb before leaving home so I'd know if anyone went into the house while we were gone."

"Back to the car," Cash demanded without asking for further explanation. "Both of you. Now."

Opa scurried ahead, but Krista couldn't seem to move. Cash grabbed her arm and rushed her down the steps and into the car.

"Is all of this really necessary?" she asked as he settled into the driver's seat.

"With a bomber after you? Absolutely." He revved the engine and whipped the vehicle down the driveway. He mounted his cell phone in a dash holder and punched a number.

"Cash." Jake's voice came over the speaker.

"I need the squad at Krista's house now." He explained the paper. "May be nothing, but I'm not taking any chances."

"Where are you now?"

"In the car. Putting some distance between us and the house."

"If it's our bomber, he could've left behind a package, and we'll need you to clear the house."

Krista gasped. She hadn't even considered a bomb could've been waiting for them.

Cash glanced at her. "I'm not leaving Krista and Otto alone. Assign someone to their protection duty and then I'll check out the house." He pulled to the curb at the entrance of a park and gave Jake their location before hanging up.

"Do you really think it's the bomber?" Opa asked from the backseat.

"So far neither one of you has come up with another threat to Krista." Cash swiveled to look at Opa, then back at Krista. "Has that changed?"

Krista shook her head and gave Opa a pointed look to stop him from saying anything about her past.

"Then, yeah, Otto," Cash said. "To answer your question, I think it's the bomber."

ELEVEN

Krista's little paper in the door finally cemented Cash's certainty. She was hiding something. An average person didn't think to take such evasive measures. Skyler would say that ongoing red flags like this one indicated Krista was involved with the bomber, but Cash still didn't buy it. He was a good judge of character, and after seeing her love and tenderness with her students and Otto, Cash couldn't reconcile that behavior with a person who would plot to kill innocent people with a bomb.

He would, however, concede that there was something more going on here, and he needed answers. Truthful ones.

"The paper in the door thing," he said, keeping his tone casual in hopes that Krista would quit staring out the car window and look at him. "How'd you know to do that?"

She glanced at him but quickly looked away. "I saw it on television."

Short and sweet her voice rang true, but he was starting to realize she looked away when she didn't want to talk to him. Not an uncommon action for someone with a secret to hide or someone who was outright lying.

"And you thought of it this morning, just like that?" he continued, hoping to draw her out.

She shrugged, not giving him the peace of mind he sought. He'd try the straightforward approach. "Krista, is there something you're not telling me?"

"I've told you everything I know about the bomb and bomber." She continued to gaze out the window.

Great. A perfect way to answer his question without really answering his question. He wanted to ask about her marriage, too, and the fact that Skyler couldn't find any record of it to see if she'd also sidestep that, but he had to respect Skyler's decision to keep that bit of research from Krista. If Skyler wasn't pulling up to the curb, he'd have a go at asking additional questions until Krista broke and told him the truth.

"Both of you wait here while I bring Skyler up-to-date." He issued a warning look that brooked no argument before climbing out and joining Skyler.

"I'd like to take your car so we don't have to move Otto," he said.

Skyler traded keys with him and held on to his hand. "Don't let this thing you've got going on with Ms. Curry distract you."

"Are you ever planning to stop calling her Ms. Curry?"

"Not as long as she's on my suspect list. Helps to keep a professional distance." Surprisingly, her voice didn't hold any censure. She squeezed his hand and let go. "Be careful. Okay?"

"I'm always careful." He smiled to ease her mind, then jogged to her car and pushed the speed limit all the way to Otto's house, where the team truck was parked at the end of the driveway. The robot they'd affectionately named Wally after the *WALL-E* movie sat on the sidewalk. It held a camera and X-ray machine for taking a first look at a suspicious package. Brady had likely wheeled it out to keep busy and now stood over it.

He looked up at Cash. "Two bomb scares in two days. That's a record for us."

"I'm not expecting to find anything here. This is just a precaution." Cash climbed into the truck. He passed Darcie sitting in the medical bay and spotted Jake in the communications suite up front. Cash dropped into a seat by the robot controls in the middle of the vehicle. Someone had already unpacked his protective bomb disposal suit and set it on a bench. Likely Brady, who trailed Cash inside and took the seat next to him. This incident didn't require a negotiator, so Archer wasn't present.

"Let me get going on the initial sweep." Cash logged his password into the computer and started Wally crawling toward the house. When the robot's caterpillar tracks clicked up the steps and stopped at the front door, Cash used the camera to scan for a booby trap. If someone set a bomb in the house, rigging the door would be an obvious choice that would also be quick and deadly for the person who stepped inside.

"Preparing to breach the door," Cash called out. He didn't see obvious signs of a booby trap, but it could be hidden and there was always the potential for an explosion.

Maneuvering Wally's arms to turn a doorknob took skill, but Cash's movements were precise. He'd used robotic tools in Afghanistan, but in addition, he, like every other bomb tech on an accredited squad in the country, had gone through the FBI's rigorous bomb tech training school in Alabama.

He held his breath, turned the knob and pushed the door open. Nothing.

Everyone in the truck let out a breath, but the search for a possible bomb wasn't over yet.

"Going in." He guided Wally over the threshold.

Inch by inch he crawled the place, looking for any obvious devices, boxes or bags. He checked doorways and windows, then double-checked kitchen cabinets, bathrooms, closets and under beds in the master and guest bedrooms. The only space he hadn't cleared was Krista's room. He had mixed emotions about looking at her personal things, but he was here to save lives not worry about his feelings.

He sent Wally rumbling forward and panned the camera under the bed.

What in the world?

He squinted at the screen and blinked hard, but the pistol tucked underneath her bed remained.

Krista had a gun. A gun! *Unbelievable.*

"Dude," Brady whispered. "Did you know about this?"

Cash was thankful for Brady's hushed tone. "No. Maybe it belongs to the intruder."

Brady rolled his eyes. "Yeah right. Why would he leave a gun behind? If he ditched it, he wouldn't do it in the house, where we could find the gun and trace it. And he's not dumb enough to want the woman he's tried to abduct to be armed."

"Regardless, keep it quiet until I can confirm if the stupid thing is even real. No sense in adding to the stress level without confirmation." *Right, that's the only reason you're not telling Jake about this.*

Fortunately, Brady nodded, and Cash finished his search.

"Initial sweep done. We're clear." He sat back and rolled his shoulders. "I'll go in and give it a once-over, but nothing looks problematic."

"Let's get you suited up." Brady grabbed the Explosive Ordinance Disposal suit and held it out.

The suit weighed around ninety pounds and had zippers and Velcro straps on the back and sides, making Brady's help a necessity.

"I'll meet you at the house after the all clear to keep you from waddling back here." Brady grinned as he settled the helmet on Cash's head.

Cash chuckled at yet one more of Brady's easygoing quips. Others thought this lighthearted side was all there was to Brady, but he had a depth that he let few people see. He came from a low-income family living in a run-down trailer and had faced all the stereotypes heaped on his head as a kid. He'd learned to joke as a way of deflecting problems.

Cash grabbed a pair of disposable gloves on the way out, earning a raise of the eyebrows from Darcie. Many people thought bomb techs wore protective gloves, but they rarely did. There was nothing more important to an EOD guy than dexterity of his fingers. One wrong move and...

Darcie was another story. She knew he didn't wear gloves, but he wasn't about to explain that he needed them to pick up a potential firearm. He stepped down from the truck and trudged toward the house. Even a hint of clear skies during the rainy season usually made him smile, but his mood was far too gloomy after finding the gun to let the sun cheer him. Inside, he scanned everywhere, remaining on alert. Even with his vigilant approach, he soon confirmed his initial assessment of everything but the gun. He snapped on the gloves and dropped to his knees by the bed. He shone his light underneath.

A pistol lay near the head of the bed.

Shoot. The thing was real, but was it Krista's?

He pulled it out and examined it. The old Colt .45 was fully loaded with a bullet chambered for quick use. Not something he'd ever recommend for gun safety reasons. He made sure the safety was engaged and laid it on the bed.

Disheartened, he went to the front door and gave Brady a thumbs-up. It would be easier if Cash had a communication device to talk to the team, but with bombs often controlled by radio-frequency devices there was no point in paying for a wireless comm unit in his helmet when he couldn't use it.

He went back to the bedroom and stared at the Colt.

What in blazes did he do about this? More important, why would Krista need a gun—a loaded one at that—at her fingertips? It sure wasn't purchased as a result of last night's attack. There was no way she could've procured a weapon since then.

And if it was as simple as owning a gun like many people did, why didn't she mention it to him after the attack? He wanted to give her the benefit of the doubt, but this omission, added to the other secrets, sent his anger firing. Granted, he had no right to know her personal business, but he was sticking his neck out for her. Was it too much to expect her to tell him she owned a gun?

Brady clapped him on the back, then removed

the helmet. "Not a good sign if she didn't tell you about it."

"You think?" Cash fired off the sarcastic comment and turned to give Brady access to the suit's many zippers. Cash wanted to jerk the quick-release toggles and rush over to Krista to demand an explanation. Thing was, if this gun was legally registered by the state where she purchased it, she had every right to have it in her home. And as long as it had nothing to do with their investigation, then even as a deputy he had no right to know why she owned it. That made him madder still.

Brady pulled a Velcro strap on the jacket. "What's Krista's story anyway? Knowing to put something in the door to warn off intruders. A gun under her bed. Sounds to me like a woman running from or scared of something."

"She says she saw the paper idea on TV. And anyway, lots of people own guns." Cash couldn't believe he was defending her. Not when he had the exact same concerns.

"Come on, man. Open your eyes. She's snowing you and you can't even see it." Brady eyed him. "Or don't you want to?"

Cash shrugged.

Brady removed the jacket and set it on the bed. "Let me at least run the gun to see if she has a carry permit."

"You might not find anything. If you remember, she said she'd just come back to town. She could have purchased the gun in Georgia and I'm not sure if they require registration or not. Since we don't require it here, if she doesn't take it out of the house, she doesn't need a carry permit and it's legit."

Brady ignored Cash and dug out his phone while Cash shed the suit pants and packed them in the case Brady had set on the floor.

Brady's conversation with records was short and to the point and Cash didn't like his buddy's gloomy expression when he disconnected. "Georgia doesn't have firearm registration, but they do require a carry permit. I'd like to request that information, and run the serial number through NCIC."

Cash didn't want to search the National Crime Information Center's database that held records of stolen weapons and ones used to commit crimes among other things. "I don't want to go there. Not yet anyway."

Brady appraised him.

"I'm not saying this because I have a thing for the woman," Cash said. "I'm saying it because once we open this door, we can't shut it."

"Meaning?"

"If we find the gun was used illegally, then we have to do more digging. Not sure it's appropriate to do that without talking to her first."

"You can ask her permission to run it."

"Why would I do that?"

"Because you're not using your head here."

Cash didn't like the fact that she might be in possession of a stolen firearm. But he also didn't like the thought of invading her privacy, or even asking her if he could run the gun's serial number, making him think Brady might be right about his motives.

"I'll be glad to ask her," Brady offered. "That way she'll be mad at me."

"I'm a big boy, Brady. I can ask if I think it's necessary."

"Probably doesn't matter. As lead investigator, Skyler's gonna question Krista about it anyway."

Cash scowled at his friend. "So why all this fuss, then?"

"Just wanted you to see you weren't thinking clearly." He raised a brow. "How'd I do with that?"

He'd been successful. More than successful. When it came to Krista, Cash had to examine his motives constantly, and Brady could help keep Cash on track going forward. Not that he'd do anything about Brady's advice, but Cash would at least be aware of his mixed motives. "You did good, man. Think you can call me out again if needed?"

Brady grinned ear to ear. "Oh, yeah, I'll call you out any day."

Cash nodded, appreciating his friend even more. He glanced at the gun one more time. He had a clear mind now. A mind that told him to be watchful. The gun might only be the first of many unsettling secrets he would learn about Krista.

TWELVE

Krista felt like a wayward child as Cash and Skyler trailed her around Opa's house while she looked for anything missing or out of place. They'd only made it through the first room, and Krista was perspiring under their scrutiny. Skyler continued to keep Krista under the microscope, but since Cash had asked about the paper in the door, he'd been looking at her funny, too.

She hadn't lied to him about it. She *had* seen the technique in a television show once, but that wasn't the whole truth. Not one to lie, she could hardly look him in the eye without flinching.

At this rate, she'd never make it through the whole house. She faced Skyler. "Isn't one of you trailing me enough?"

Skyler stared at Krista for a few moments, then held up her hands. "I'll step out."

"No, wait! That's not what I…" Krista let her words fall off as Cash cocked an eyebrow. "Never mind." She went back to work.

"You got this?" Skyler asked Cash.

"Yeah," he responded. "Maybe you should take

Otto to the fire station while we do the search. He looked pretty beat last I saw him on the porch, and he could rest on our couch. I'll bring Krista over once we're done here. We can all sit down to talk about how to make sure this doesn't happen again."

When Skyler didn't respond, Krista turned to look. Skyler's gaze was fixed on Cash. Maybe Skyler was wondering if it was a good idea to bring Krista into their home.

Cash seemed to have no such concern. "C'mon, Skyler. Otto's sick. He needs rest and he's not going to get it here with all the commotion going on."

Skyler chewed on her lip and glanced at the door. Krista had seen Skyler's compassionate side and suspected Skyler wanted to do what was best for Opa as long as it didn't compromise her investigation.

"Fine," she finally said. "I'll take him and assign Brady to oversee the forensic team. You can continue to supervise Ms. Curry's review of the property."

Krista felt like a fraud. She'd wanted Skyler to call her Ms. Curry, but the name rang false each time, and as Krista got to know this team, it bothered her. Still, she wasn't ready to tell them her real name.

She forced out a smile and called over her

shoulder as she headed for the door, "I'll just say goodbye to Opa."

When Krista returned to her search, Skyler stepped outside and closed the door. Without looking, Krista felt Cash move closer. She could smell the clean, fresh scent she'd come to associate with him and wished he'd back off.

She wanted his protection—needed his protection—but after this incident, he was bound to stick even closer to her. She couldn't handle the stress of this emotionally charged chemistry between them on top of everything else. It was high time they got it all out in the open. She turned, catching him by surprise, and he bumped into her. He gripped her elbow. She took a hasty step back and nearly tripped over a footstool.

"You're sure jumpy." He carefully watched her.

"I wanted you to leave instead of Skyler."

"I'd have to be blind not to have noticed that." His lips tipped in his trademark cocky smile. She should find his attitude irritating, but it had the opposite effect on her.

She took another step back for good measure. "It's this thing between us. The chemistry or whatever you want to call it. I'm not in a place for a relationship right now and it's making me uncomfortable."

"Afraid you can't resist me, huh?" he joked.

"I'm serious here, Cash. I can't deal with it,

and I want to make it perfectly clear that this isn't going anywhere."

His jaw tightened for a moment, then a thin smile claimed his mouth. "I get it. Hands off. All business. Just what I want, too."

"You seem mad."

"Mad? No. I'm good." He gestured at the hall. "Let's get back to the job at hand."

She went to work, but even after sharing her feelings, she remained uncomfortable under his scrutiny. Not only because of his intense study, but also because her mind kept going to her escape bag in the crawl space. It was well hidden, and she wasn't worried about them discovering it today, but she had a strong urge to grab the bag and run.

She entered her bedroom and saw her gun lying on the bed.

Oh, no. How had she not realized he'd find the gun on his sweep of the house? She could have prepared an explanation instead of standing here looking suspicious.

"Is that your gun?" His tone was casual, as if they were talking about the weather instead of a loaded pistol.

She flashed a look at him, saw the steely resolve in his eyes, his rock-hard expression. Withholding the truth would be a mistake.

"It belonged to my dad. I keep it for protection." She faked a laugh. "You know, single girl and all that."

"You have a permit for the gun?"

"No, I mean…he gave it to me so I… Do I need one?"

"Depends on where your dad bought it and if you ever take it out of the house."

"It stays here," she said, keeping to what she was certain of. "Is that a problem?"

"No. The only permit you need in Oregon is to carry a gun outside your home." He eyed her, his expression begging her to offer additional information.

"Funny story," she said to dodge his curiosity. "Did you know the law *requires* you to own a gun in Kennesaw?"

"What?" He laughed, just as she'd hoped.

She smiled back. "I'm not joking. If you live in the city limits, the law requires the head of households to own a gun. Keeps crime down."

He scrunched his brows together.

"Look it up online if you don't believe me."

"Trust me, I will." His lighthearted tone gave way to another suspicious look. "You didn't mention your father's name."

No, of course she hadn't. She never mentioned him if she could help it. He was in prison, and she didn't want to be tied to him, but Cash would dig if she didn't respond.

"Max Nealy." The bogus name her father had taken when they'd moved to Georgia came much easier to her lips than his actual last name. He'd chosen a different last name from her so if he was arrested he wouldn't drag her into his mess. Now it could make it harder for Cash to locate her father.

Before Cash could ask anything else about her past, she turned her focus as quickly as she could to finishing her inspection.

"Nothing's missing or disturbed," she said, keeping her gaze on the ransacked room.

"Don't you find that odd?" Cash asked. "Someone enters your house, but nothing's taken?"

"I don't know what to think." She turned to get a read on his thoughts "You seem to find it odd, though."

He nodded. "Why go through all the trouble and risk exposure to break into your house, then do nothing? Makes no sense."

"Then maybe we *are* missing something. If so, it's not obvious to me."

He rubbed his jaw, his gaze a million miles away.

"What are you thinking?"

"That I don't have enough experience here. Let's go pick up Otto, and we can run this past Skyler and the other team members."

Cash led the way out of the house and stopped next to Brady, who was talking to Veronica, the same forensic tech from last night.

"We're heading to the firehouse," Cash said. "You good here?"

Brady nodded, then looked at Krista. "I'll need your keys to lock up."

Right, she was leaving him in charge of her home. She hadn't thought of that. Hadn't thought of Brady being in Opa's house alone with access to every nook and cranny. Access to the crawl space. "You know, on second thought, I think it's a good idea if I stay to lock up. Maybe Veronica will find something that you'll want to talk to me about. Plus, Opa's very particular about his house." She spoke the truth. Still, it felt like a lie.

Cash's eyebrows shot up but not faster than Brady's.

"This situation is my fault," she said quickly. "I already hate that I've disturbed Opa's peaceful sanctuary and if I stay, I can help ensure nothing else is moved or changed. I'll go sit on the couch while you do your thing." She retreated to the house and heard footsteps jogging up behind her.

"I'll keep you company," Cash offered.

"If you like," she said pleasantly, but she knew the next few hours would be some of the longest of her life.

Krista followed Cash across the firehouse's polished concrete floors. They stepped through a large open bay area that was once home to the fire trucks and into a huge family room with air ducts and plumbing running above. A spicy, mouthwatering aroma came from the open kitchen, where

Darcie was preparing the meal that Cash had offered to share with her and Opa while they discussed the break-in.

"If you want any food, you'd better pick up your speed," Brady called over his shoulder as he charged through the kitchen.

"Better listen to him," Darcie warned, but she had a smile on her face. "I made my famous enchiladas and he's not apt to leave any on the plate."

Cash shook his head and led her to a dining room with a long table and chairs for twelve. Plain white plates ringed the table and platters with cheesy enchiladas, rice and corn sat in the middle.

"About time." Brady winked from his seat next to Opa. Jake sat at the end of the table and Darcie dropped onto a chair on the other end.

"We have left seats open for you." Opa grinned and pointed at two available chairs next to Skyler.

Krista didn't need to be a rocket scientist to figure out Opa wanted her to sit with Cash. She made a mental note to tell Opa to back off his obvious matchmaking when they got home.

"Let's say grace before we pass the food." Darcie gestured for everyone to link hands, and the team members silently complied.

Interesting. The entire team prayed together. Not a common thing in law enforcement, Krista suspected. After the amen, food seemed to fly from platters and onto plates as teammates talked over each other and laughed at puny jokes. Opa smiled through all of it and even took more food than he'd been eating of late. Despite the stress, this was turning out to be good for him.

In a lull, she heard someone fumbling with the front doorknob. She shot a look in that direction, but she couldn't see the entryway.

"Relax." Skyler's eyes sparkled like a child's on Christmas. "That'll be Logan."

Cash leaned closer. "Her fiancé."

"I should move. He'll want to sit here." Krista started to get up.

"Please, don't." Cash stopped her. "They spend enough time hanging all over each other. We could all use the break. Right, guys?"

"Isn't that the truth," Jake grumbled.

"Amen to that," Archer added, then the others started laughing.

Skyler shook her head and looked at Brady. "You made sure Veronica covered everything?"

"Subtle change of subject, Skyler," Darcie said. "Real subtle."

"I wasn't trying to be subtle." Skyler peered at Brady.

His mouth bulging with enchiladas, he nodded.

"This whole break-in seems odd, doesn't it?" Archer asked as he salted his corn. "If the bomber didn't rig the place to blow and didn't steal anything, what was the point of it all?"

"I've been wondering the same thing," Cash

said as Krista heard the front door close in the background.

Skyler shifted in her seat, likely in anticipation. "What if he was looking for something?"

Jake looked up from scooping rice onto his plate. "Then the place would have been tossed, but it wasn't even disturbed."

"If it was the guy who's been tailing her," Skyler said, "then he would know the house was empty, giving him plenty of time to perform a neat search."

"But why? He'd already broken in last night. There's no point in hiding the fact that he came back," Brady suggested before stuffing another bite of cheesy tortilla into his mouth.

"I'm wondering what he could possibly want," Krista stated in case they thought she had any idea of what this intruder was looking for.

Brady swallowed, his gaze locked on her. "That seems pretty obvious to me. He was looking for something you have that could incriminate him."

"Incriminate him?" The words flew out before Krista could control her tone. "What would I have that could incriminate a bomber?"

Brady kept his focus on her. "Plenty of things if you're working with him."

Her mouth fell open, and she didn't know what to say.

"With all of you riding her case, if she possessed something incriminating, wouldn't she have already turned it over by now?" a man Krista suspected was Logan asked from the doorway.

All eyes turned to him. He stood tall in a well-tailored suit, white shirt and striped tie.

"You don't even know what we're talking about, Suit," Brady fired back, but there was humor in his tone.

Cash glanced at Krista. "He's FBI."

"Haven't you learned yet, Brady?" Logan rested his hands on Skyler's shoulders. "Feds know everything."

The group groaned in unison.

"Seriously," he said after the noise died down. "My sweetie here filled me in." He bent and kissed the top of her head. "Hi, honey."

She smiled up at him. "Hi back at you."

"You were saying, Logan?" Jake asked, bringing everyone back.

"Right." Logan nodded. "Skyler brought me up to speed on the investigation, and I heard enough of the discussion on my way in to give my opinion. Like I said, if she had something that could be used to catch this guy, I think she'd have turned it over to you by now."

Brady dropped his fork to his plate with a clang. "Krista could be hanging back to see how this goes down. If charges are brought, then she'll use this item to plea-bargain her way to lesser charges."

"Your theory makes no sense," Cash said. "If

it incriminates the bomber, it will most likely incriminate her, too. Wouldn't she get rid of it?"

"Not necessarily." Brady eyed Cash.

"Then why the abduction attempt last night? Why not just sneak in and let her sleep while looking for this supposed item?"

"*She's* the one who said she was sleeping and that the man tried to abduct her. No one else saw it."

"I heard her scream, man. It was bloodcurdling. Not something she could fake." Cash was breathing hard and Krista saw him draw a deep, cleansing breath. "I'm concerned the bomber stopped by today to scope the place out so he could do a better job of abducting her. Maybe even kill her."

Krista gasped.

"Sorry I was so blunt but it had to be said." Cash swiveled in his chair. "I'd like to recommend that you and Otto spend the night here."

Opa shook his head. "I won't be run out of my own home, Cash Dixon, but you're more than welcome to stay with us."

"If that's the only way to make sure you're safe, then that's what I'll do."

"You sure, man?" Brady shot Cash a pointed look.

Cash crossed his arms and stared back at Brady. "I'm positive."

"What about work?" Brady fired back.

Cash looked at Jake. "I'll be taking a few vacation days. Sorry for the short notice, but no one is getting to Krista or Otto. Not on my watch."

THIRTEEN

Krista stopped in Opa's room to kiss him good-night. He was propped up in his bed, his Bible in his hands, doing his nightly devotions. Peace that made no sense after the recent chaos in their lives shone in his eyes.

He patted the side of his bed. "Come tell me why you have such a long face, Liebchen."

"Just tired." She sat next to him.

"It is more than tired, I suspect. You are upset about the day's events and that is understandable." He took her hand in his, his wrinkled skin feeling familiar and comforting. "There is good news. Reporters are hailing you as a hero for stopping the bombing."

"For now, but when—"

He lifted a finger to his lips. "Shh, no sense in worrying about what might happen."

He had a point. One she wished she could embrace, but her history warned her to be cautious. "At least they haven't found where we live yet. Though I imagine it's just a matter of time. Then the harassment will start again."

He watched her, his wizened eyes assessing. "Would you like to pray with me that God will resolve this quickly?"

She shook her head. "It's late, and you need your sleep."

"Ah, so you are running from God again, I see."

"Not running so much as not trusting Him to take care of us." She paused to gather her thoughts so she didn't accidently say something that would offend Opa's faith. "Every time I do trust God, He puts a problem in my life so big I never fully recover from it."

"He has a reason for allowing this new trouble in your life, Liebchen, and for all the troubles that came before."

"So you always say. Problem is, He's not telling me why."

"I suspect," Opa said, pausing and intensifying his eye contact, "God is trying to get your attention, but only you can know that for sure."

She wished God's reasons were ever that obvious. "Sounds so simple when you say it, but honestly, I don't think He's hearing me."

"He is listening. Trust me on that. You might have to dig deep to find the answer you seek."

"Again, easier said than done."

"There is nothing easy about being a Christian, Liebchen." He patted her hand. "Take some time to look beyond this situation to see why God is allowing this in your life. You will see. It will become clear."

She didn't think Opa was right, but because she loved him, she would take time tonight to explore the possibility. He'd never steered her wrong—except with Toby.

"I love you, Opa." She gave him a quick but sincere hug, then sat back.

"And I love you, Liebchen." He smiled at her. "Now go entertain Cash so he does not die of boredom in my family room."

She sighed at his obvious attempt to push her together with Cash, but with Opa's happy mood, she didn't have the heart to tell him to back off.

She went to talk to Cash even though she didn't feel like entertaining him. Okay, maybe she didn't really dislike the idea, which was why she'd simply check on him to be sure he had everything he needed to spend the night on the couch, then she'd head to her room.

Instead, he somehow managed to get her to sit down and he started sharing fascinating stories about the FRS. Stories of rescues, of saving lives and of losing others. His passion and commitment to his team and to helping people was alive in his voice. His face was animated, his body relaxed as if comfortable in his skin. She was drawn to him in a new way and wanted to sit right there, talking the night away. Getting to know him on a much deeper level.

"I'm the newest guy on the squad," he continued. "But in a lot of ways it feels like we've been together for years."

"I imagine your Delta team was a lot like that, too," she offered, hoping he'd share that part of his past, as well.

He nodded, but the enthusiasm that had lit him from inside vanished.

"Was it hard to leave them?" she prodded, hoping to regain that connection they'd been sharing.

"Yeah." He looked at his watch and came to his feet. "It's getting late. We have to be up early."

"Of course." She stood and tried not to let him know his evasiveness hurt. "I'll see you in the morning."

Behind closed doors, she shook her head. Here she'd been thinking the worst thing she could do was sit down and talk to Cash, opening the door for something to happen between them and encouraging him to dig into her past. Then he'd clammed up and had all but thrown her from the room and now she thought *that* was the worst thing.

Not hardly. The worst thing was her certainty that he was hiding something big. Something that could rock her world again if she let herself trust him.

No way would she go there. Not on a personal level or with the investigation. She respected him for standing up for her, but it could all be an act.

She'd seen that before. One cop playing the good cop role. Earning her trust, then using everything she'd said against her.

No, she would never fall for that again.

The next morning, Cash stationed himself in a position to see the playground and parking lot while still keeping a view of Krista's classroom through the window. He took out his phone and searched the internet to see if heads of households in Kennesaw were required to own a gun. Took only a minute to discover Krista had told the truth. Not surprising. No one could make up such an outrageous story on the fly. Especially not someone like Krista, who seemed to have a difficult time hiding her discomfort when she didn't want to answer questions.

Too bad her truthfulness didn't improve his mood. He'd spent the night on alert and he was exhausted and cranky. Didn't help that Krista kept looking at him as if she wanted an explanation for why he'd clammed up last night.

He glanced into the classroom and watched her move among the children. Last night's conversation came rushing back. It had felt so natural and effortless between them. He'd never known such ease with a woman. He'd even wanted to tell her about the loss of his team. To talk about it with someone for the first time. Surprised him. He didn't, of course. He'd clammed up instead.

Telling her would push him over that personal line he was trying not to cross with her. The line she'd said herself that she didn't want him to cross. Best to stay focused on her protection detail.

The wind kicked up, and he hunched into his jacket as he walked the perimeter. When he spotted Skyler's SUV pull into the parking lot, he was glad for the distraction.

He met her at the playground fence. "What brings you here?"

"We located one of the men from the stadium video," she said excitedly. "I'd like to arrange a lineup for Krista."

The good news lifted some of Cash's crankiness. "I'm sure she'd be glad to do it after her shift. I can ask on her next break."

Her eyes narrowed, Skyler moved closer. "I was hoping if I talked to Krista, I could get her to come in now."

"You can ask, but she's dedicated to these kids. I doubt she'll leave them."

"I suspected as much, but it would be a good idea to get going on this lead."

His gut clenched at her dire tone. "Why the rush?"

"Our warrant came through for the black SUV's rental car records. We ran a background check on the driver. He's a virtual ghost. His ID is for a man who died years ago."

A bad feeling settled over Cash and he glanced

into the classroom to make sure Krista was okay. "Getting a fake ID issued means he's connected and has more skills than we first considered."

Skyler nodded. "I hate to say this, but it's classic behavior for a terrorist."

Cash shot her a look. "That's a pretty big leap, isn't it? There are plenty of other cons out there who assume identities."

"True, but how many of them plant bombs?"

"Okay, so let's suppose for a minute that this bomb was the work of a terrorist. Why hasn't he taken credit? Even if the bomb failed, it's a perfect opportunity to get his message out to the public and drum up fear. Plus, terrorists are known for their suicide missions. Why not this guy?"

"Good questions."

"But you don't sound like you think they're valid."

"Oh, they're valid, all right. I just don't have the answers." She scowled. "The only ID we have is for a guy whose past is a dead end, so there's not much we can do about him."

"Maybe there's a link between him and the suspect from the video."

"We're working on it, but nothing has popped up yet. This is why I wanted to get Krista to do the lineup ASAP." Skyler massaged the base of her neck.

Tension. Just as everyone else involved in the investigation experienced, but being lead investigator for County, Skyler had to feel the stress more than others. Cash wished he could alleviate it, but there was nothing he could do.

She looked around the area, her gaze assessing and focused. "I'd thought your self-imposed protection detail for Krista was an overreaction."

"But now?" Cash asked, not liking her tone.

She made strong eye contact. "Now I recommend you step up your game and assume full-alert status before a tragedy strikes."

FOURTEEN

"Thanks for coming, Ms. Curry," Skyler said as she moved toward the window overlooking a small room where six men would soon file in for a lineup.

Krista could hardly stomach the thought of seeing the bomber, but she also wanted him to be in the lineup so she could identify him and end this turmoil.

She glanced into the room. The bomber. He'd be right there. In mere moments. His cold, gray eyes and ugly scowl directed at her again.

Her body started to tremble, and she wrapped her arms around her stomach in self-preservation.

"Hey." Cash stepped up next to her and rested a hand on her shoulder. "They won't be able to see you."

"I know. It's just… I… Seeing him…" The trembling increased.

Cash leaned in. "I'm here for you, honey," he whispered. "It'll be okay."

Honey. He'd called her honey. She liked the way it sounded and would like to take time to think about it, but not now. Not when thoughts of the men behind the window consumed her mind.

The men.

She took a deep, shuttering breath and let it out. Cash moved closer. She felt the warmth of his body. Heard the confidence in his tone. He was there for her as he'd been since she'd met him. Her apprehension lessened a fraction and she found enough courage to move on. "Let's do this."

Skyler requested the men to file in, then turned to Krista. "This is going to be hard and your first response will be to hurry through the line, but take your time. Look carefully at each man. If you want to see them from different angles, just ask and I'll have them comply. Okay?"

Krista nodded and clasped her hands together.

One by one, they stepped in—all men fitting the bomber's size and weight. The officer instructed them to turn and Krista swallowed hard. She forced herself to focus. Let her gaze run quickly over them.

He's not here. A wave of relief washed through her, before she remembered Skyler's warning and her heart plummeted. She looked again. Carefully. Her breath held, she swept her gaze over them, then locked on their faces. Their eyes. One man after another.

"I'm sorry." Disappointment brought tears to her eyes and she had to bite her lip to keep her cool. "None of them are the bomber."

"You're sure?" Skyler asked.

Krista nodded. "I'd recognize him even in my sleep. These guys might be similar in build, but their eyes are all wrong."

"Okay, then." Skyler dismissed the men before turning back to Krista. "We're still trying to find the other man from the security footage, but I don't hold out much hope of locating him."

"If you do, I'll be glad to view another lineup."

"Thank you for your cooperation." Skyler smiled sincerely. "I know it took guts to look at these guys. I appreciate your willingness to help."

Krista returned the smile with a wobbly one of her own. She got the feeling that Skyler was finally looking more favorably upon her. She faced Cash. "We should get going. Opa's likely wondering where we are."

"Can I have a quick word with you, Cash?" Skyler asked.

"I'll wait in the hallway." Krista stepped outside and leaned against the wall. She hadn't closed the door, but as hard as she tried, she couldn't make out the conversation between Skyler and Cash until he suddenly raised his voice.

"Priceless, Skyler. Just priceless," he exclaimed. "Krista comes in at your request, then you don't believe her because you think she's protecting the bomber? Unbelievable."

Well, then. So much for Skyler's favorable thoughts.

"We have to look at all possibilities," Skyler replied. "I want to believe her, but I wouldn't be doing my job if I didn't caution you."

"*You* might have to look at all possibilities, but *I* don't."

"Cash, wait," Skyler said.

Without giving a response, or at least one Krista could hear, Cash stomped toward her. She pushed off the wall and waited for him.

"C'mon. Let's get out of here." Without another word, he took long, pounding strides down the hallway in silence. The car ride to Erwin's house was made in silence. Tense, uncomfortable silence. She'd hoped Opa would lighten things up with his usual good humor, but even he couldn't get Cash to talk.

Krista honestly regretted the position she'd put him in with Skyler. Krista wanted to be angry with Skyler, but she really *was* just doing her job, as she'd told Cash. She was nothing like the detectives on Toby's case. She might have Krista firmly lodged on her suspect list, but she didn't treat her like dirt or tell the press that she suspected Krista's involvement. That was a huge win in Krista's book.

Cash remained distracted as he parked outside Opa's house, leaving Krista to help Opa out of the car.

"Bad day?" he whispered and stared at Cash,

who stood at attention by his door, his gaze searching the surrounding area.

"I'll tell you about it later," Krista replied and concentrated on helping Opa climb the stairs to the porch. Cash followed in silence.

He suddenly rushed past them and blocked the way. "The front door's open."

Krista's gaze flew to the door. He was right—it was cracked open an inch.

Not again.

"Stay here while I check it out." Cash pulled his weapon and elbowed the door.

She glanced at Opa and found unease in his eyes. The same anxiety raced through her. A loud thud sounded from inside. Her gut said to flee. She swallowed down her fear and stepped to the door to see if Cash was okay.

The sofa was turned over and a table lay on its side in the family room. Opa's lovely books had been dropped like trash to the floor. She caught movement deeper in the room. Cash was struggling with a man wearing a ski mask. They wrestled. Back and forth. Cash winning at times, the intruder others. The intruder suddenly broke free and grabbed Opa's favored ceramic stein from Germany. He raised it over Cash's head.

Fear for his safety took her breath but she managed to shout, "Look out, Cash!"

She hoped he heard. Didn't matter if he did. She

was too late and the stein made a sickening thud on his skull. He dropped to the floor.

The intruder spun. Took one look at her and charged.

"He's coming, Opa! Quick—move to the other side of the house." She nudged him into action and thought to follow. But this was her chance to help. She took a stance and planned to trip the man when he stepped outside.

"I'm not going without you." Opa planted his feet.

"I'll be right after you." She pushed him again.

He took a few steps, then stopped to wait for her.

The intruder was almost upon them. No time for either of them to flee.

She stepped between Opa and the threat. She shot out a foot. Unsettled the intruder. He staggered for a second but regained his footing faster than she'd expected and tried to grab her arm.

She jumped back. He stumbled to the side but quickly recovered. She took a stance learned in her self-defense courses and blocked his forward movement with her fists. He kept coming. She readjusted and blocked him again.

"Back off," Cash shouted as he came barreling out the door. He dived at the guy. Missed and hit the porch floor with a solid thud.

The intruder bolted down the steps.

"Stay here," Cash commanded as he staggered to his feet.

He charged after the man, but his steps were unsteady. He stumbled again. Righted himself and held on to a tree. Took a few more steps and grabbed another tree.

Krista hated to see Cash fighting a lost cause when the guy was long gone.

She jogged down the steps and laid a hand on his arm. "He's gone."

"I know, but I…"

"I get that you want to go after him, but you're clearly dizzy."

He tried to stand unaided, then leaned against the tree. His eyes had lost their determination.

"You're bleeding." Krista tried to touch his head, but he backed away. "Let's go sit down."

He swept fingers across the injury and winced. "Not in the house. It's a crime scene. We'll sit in the car."

"Okay." She tried to help him to the vehicle.

He shrugged off her hand and made his way only to lean against the hood. He pulled out his phone. "I'll call Jake and get an alert out."

She nodded. "I'll go get Opa."

He was already climbing down the stairs and met her at the bottom.

"Cash says we shouldn't go back inside yet. We'll sit in the car until his team arrives."

"I hope Darcie comes along." He tipped his

head at Cash. "Looks like Cash could use her attention."

"I saw the creep hit him with your stein, but, of course, Cash won't admit he needs to sit down. If we sit, maybe he will, too." She escorted Opa to the car and got him settled in the back. She didn't say anything to Cash but took her seat in the front. He didn't join them.

"He's stubborn," Krista mumbled.

"As are you, my Liebchen."

She cast Opa a stern look, and he chuckled. A few minutes later Cash dropped onto the front seat.

"Are you feeling less dizzy?" she asked.

"I'm fine."

"I do not understand what is happening, Cash," Opa said. "This person—maybe the bomber—has been here three times now. Once to steal away my Krista. The second like a mouse in the night, disturbing nothing. Third, like a whirling tornado, making a mess and trying to grab Krista again. What can he be after?"

Cash swiveled on the seat. He closed his eyes for a moment, likely because he was still dizzy and trying to regain his equilibrium. "With the way the house is trashed today, it tells us he's desperate to retrieve something and he no longer cares if we know about it."

"But what?" Krista asked. "I don't have anything he could want."

"And why has he tried to abduct her?"

"My guess, though you can never know what a creep like this wants, is that he thinks if he takes Krista he can force her to tell him where the thing he's looking for is located."

She looked at Cash. "Force. As in torture?"

He nodded and visions of the bomber taking control of her sent the blood draining from her face.

"Don't worry." Cash took her hand. "I won't let him get to you."

She appreciated his support and, honestly, she felt he was more than competent, but the man had almost grabbed her today. How would Cash stop such a thing in the future?

She heard the low rumble of a truck barreling down the driveway. Her pulse shot into overdrive as she swiveled to see the FRS coming to their rescue. A wave of relief over their arrival washed over her. An astounding change when she'd been so terrified to be interviewed by them at the stadium.

They climbed from the car to meet the squad, minus Archer, and the irony of Krista's situation had her shaking her head. She still feared they'd turn on her as the detectives had in Toby's investigation, but she'd come to rely on these men and women, too. And appreciate their strength and determination.

Darcie rushed up to Krista. "Are you okay? Cash told us the guy grabbed you."

"I'm fine. It's Cash you should be looking at. He was hit over the head with a heavy stein."

Darcie turned to frown at Cash, who was leaning heavily on the hood. "You didn't say anything about it when you called this in."

"That's because I'm fine."

"C'mon." Darcie grabbed his wrist as she might a wayward child. "I'll decide if you're fine or not." She dragged him toward their truck.

"Cash's gonna get an earful." Brady smiled. "Glad I'm not the one who got hurt and didn't tell her."

Jake looked at Krista. "Have you had a chance to look through the house?"

"No. Cash wanted us to wait for forensics."

Jake raised a brow but said nothing.

Krista's apprehension skyrocketed. "What aren't you telling me?"

"Cash was right. We don't want to contaminate the scene, but I suspect his real reason for staying outside is to keep you from spending more time than necessary in the mess he described on the phone."

"Unfortunately, you'll have to walk through the house to tell us if anything is missing," Brady added, his tone warmer than it had been in the past.

"We'll be by your side as you take a tour." Skyler offered a rare smile. "You ready?"

"I am coming, too," Opa said. "It is time I see just what type of man we are dealing with."

At the door, Jake handed out booties to cover their shoes, and he snapped on a pair of latex gloves, as did Skyler. Krista put on her own booties, then helped Opa.

Skyler faced Krista and Opa. "You'll want to pick things up and put them back where they belong, but please don't touch anything until after Veronica clears them. Just try to make a running inventory in your mind as you go. Call out if you notice something missing. Okay?"

"We'll do our best." Krista linked her arm in Opa's, and after the team members entered the house, she stepped over the threshold.

She'd caught a peek at the place earlier, but she'd been focused on Cash. Now she took a long look. The book she'd left on the table this morning lay on the floor next to the sheets Cash had slept in. Opa's afghan pooled under his favorite chair, the cushion ripped free and flung across the room.

The full force of what this man was capable of hit her. What if they'd been home? The monster could have— No, she wouldn't go there.

"We can do this, Liebchen," Opa encouraged.

Forcing her shoulders back, she moved forward, Opa right by her side. "This reminds me of the other time," he whispered.

Krista knew he meant after Toby's murder,

when Opa's home had been turned upside down and vandalized with threatening graffiti, leading to an ugly confrontation with her neighbors. That had served as the final straw after months of accusations and had sent Krista running from Portland.

"At least there aren't horrible messages painted on the walls this time," she whispered back.

Opa spun to face her. "But this is different, is it not? This is not the work of neighbors who took their information from the television. Nothing has been leaked to the press in this investigation. These men and women who have stood by us are honorable, Liebchen. You can trust them."

"Trust who?" Cash asked as he stepped through the door.

"I see Darcie has bandaged you up." Krista quickly changed the subject.

"I didn't need it. I let her put the dressing on, or she would never have released me."

"I heard that." Darcie came up behind him and flicked his shoulder. "If you didn't already have a bump on your head I'd give you one."

The team slipped into one of their silly moods, something Krista suspected they engaged in often to relieve the stress of their intense jobs. They really were an amazing group, as Opa had said. Could she trust them? She wanted to. Especially Cash.

Veronica entered the room carrying her large

case. "Aha. I knew you guys goofed around on the job. Now I have proof."

They groaned in unison, but it was followed by genuine smiles. Despite the situation, Krista felt herself smiling, too.

"You should do that more often," Cash said, grabbing her attention again. He let his gaze linger, seeming as if he liked what he saw.

She felt a blush creep up her neck.

"Not only is he a good man," Opa announced not too quietly. "But he cares about you."

"Yeah, he does," Brady said, but didn't sound happy about it.

Krista ignored everyone, including Opa, and continued through the family room inch by messy inch. A thorough search proved nothing was missing, so she moved on to the kitchen. Opa's irreplaceable stoneware from Germany was shattered and mixed with his favorite coffee on the floor.

Her heart ached from the trouble she'd brought to his life, but she kept moving, sifting through the mess until there was nothing else to look at. She dreaded moving on to Opa's room, where he'd already gone to assess the damage, but she wanted to help him if needed.

She found him, Bible in hand, his usual peaceful expression on his face. He looked up. "We will have a bit of work to do tonight."

She went to him, hugged him close and held

on for dear life. "I'm so sorry, Opa. I brought this mess into your life again."

"There is no reason to be sorry." He pushed back, his expression telling her he was taking this in stride like everything else. "You did not do this just like you did not kill Toby, and I will not have you feel any guilt." He tipped her chin up. "Do you hear me, Liebchen? Do not feel bad. These are just possessions. As long as my Bible has survived and you are unharmed, I am fine."

He stood up taller. "Now you go check your room and I will be with Cash in the family room."

Feeling better, she went straight to her room. She dropped to the floor to look under the bed, where she'd returned the gun after the previous break-in.

The gun. It was gone.

Stunned, she sat back. Having a gun had given her a sense of security. Now her only form of protection was gone.

No. She had Cash. He would stand by them. If nothing else, he'd proved his trustworthiness in that area. But what if the intruder came back with the same gun and used it on Cash?

She couldn't expose him to such danger. She had to tell him, but how? How did she explain that a potential kidnapper, likely a deadly bomber, was in possession of her gun and could harm others with it?

Taking her time to put off the inevitable, she

finished searching her room, then went back to the family room and faced the team. She met their gazes and Opa's squarely. "My gun is missing."

Cash grimaced but said nothing.

Skyler frowned. "All we can do at this point is make sure it's added to the stolen weapons database. Is there anything else missing?"

"Not that I can see, but I won't know for sure until I put this place back together."

"I did not notice anything, either," Opa added.

"Then since we're done here, we'll get out of your way so you can clean up," Skyler said. "Make sure you call me if you discover anything or if you happen to locate the gun."

"Coming, Cash?" Brady asked pointedly.

"I'm staying." Cash's shoulders went up in a hard line. "They need me even more than before."

Krista didn't like the reason Cash had to stay, but she was glad he wasn't leaving. He closed the door after his team and smiled, but the strain of the day hung in his eyes. "Why don't we get the furniture turned over so Otto can sit down?"

Krista nodded. "And then I'll work on his bedroom."

"I am not invisible, you know," Opa grumbled. "I can work on my own room if you will be so kind as to lift my mattress back onto the frame."

"Sure." Cash smiled sincerely this time.

They made quick work of putting his mattress back into position, and then Opa shooed them out of the room. They walked back to the family room in silence, and Cash stood at the entrance, surveying the mess as if he didn't know where to start.

"The sofa is taking up a lot of space," Krista said softly. "We should move it first."

They each took an end and flipped it over. Something shiny dropped out, bounced on the floor and slid under the coffee table. Cash went to retrieve it while Krista moved on. She righted an end table and heard Cash mumble something under his breath.

"Did you say something?" she asked, turning to look at him.

Scowling, he pulled a latex glove from his pocket and reached under the table. A metal object lay in his palm, and he stared at it. He suddenly looked up at her, his expression stony.

"What is it?" Krista held her breath for more bad news.

He met her gaze, his eyes dark and angry. "Do you recognize this?"

She started at the shiny metal tube with a black cap at the end. "I have no idea what that is."

He ground his teeth for a moment. "It's a piece of a detonator. For a bomb. If you're not involved with the bomber, why would you have something like this in your home?"

FIFTEEN

Krista watched Cash pace the floor. Back and forth. Back and forth. Part of her couldn't believe after the time they'd spent together and the relationship that seemed to be developing between them—despite their best efforts to avoid it—that he could possibly think she was involved in the bombing.

The other part of her, the one who'd lived in a state of unease for years, had expected this kind of reaction all along. Her life had come full circle. The police believed her guilty of another crime she hadn't committed. But the hurt was exponentially bigger coming from Cash. She had to get him to see she didn't know about the detonator.

She clutched his arm, forcing him to stop and look at her. "I had nothing to do with this. Please believe me."

"The evidence speaks for itself." He held up the detonator. "This is very similar to the one used in the stadium bomb."

"Similar but not an exact match?"

"Not exact, but come on, Krista. It's a detonator for a bomb. Not a run of the mill item found in someone's sofa."

She let her gaze travel the room, looking for something, anything to explain her situation. "You said yourself that you think the bomber is the one who broke in here and is targeting me. Maybe he planted that thing under the sofa to discredit me. You know, so even if I identified him, no one will believe me."

"You heard it fall out of the sofa, right?"

"Even better to make me look guilty. Put it inside the sofa and tip it over so it seems like it just happens to fall out." She waited for him to agree but he simply stared at her. "It obviously was a good idea. It's clearly working."

Cash rolled down his glove to encase the detonator and shoved it in his pocket before looking at her. "What else can I think?"

"I don't know—maybe that you've spent time with me the last few days. Gotten to know me and know I'd never do anything like this."

He eyed her for a moment. "Or," Cash said, his voice hard, "it could also be the more obvious answer. You could be the bomber's accomplice or, worse, the actual bomber. Maybe you made the bomb in this very room and the detonator slipped into the sofa unnoticed."

His comment sent her taking a step back in shock. "What about the attacks on me? This ransacking? Why would I do that? *How* could I do it? You've been with me the whole time."

His confidence faltered for a moment but quickly returned. "For starters, you could have hired someone for the break-ins to throw the investigation off track." He fisted his hands, then released them and crossed his powerful arms as if he didn't know what to do with himself. "Either way, I have to report finding this to Skyler. She'll want to bring forensics back out here for a more detailed search for bomb-making supplies and residue to see if we can match anything to the stadium bomb." He dug out his phone and started to walk away.

She grabbed his hand, threaded her fingers in his. "Please, don't call her. They won't find anything. I promise."

He stared at her. "Give me a good reason not to tell her."

Krista couldn't tell him about her past. About why she feared being targeted for the crime as had happened with Toby. The last thing she could do after this discovery was to tell him how she'd never been cleared of another serious crime.

"One reason, Krista. Just one," he pleaded, sounding desperate to believe her.

She couldn't risk exposing her past. Looking away, she said, "I don't have one."

"I didn't think so." He pulled his hand free.

She clamped her mouth closed before she thought better of her decision and spilled her guts.

"Have a seat. Skyler and Veronica will be back here soon. You'd better hope they don't find anything else."

The front door opened and Skyler stepped inside with Veronica. Opa must have heard the car pull up because he wandered out of his room. He took one look at Krista and came to sit next to her. He scooped up her hand, and she explained the situation.

"My granddaughter is not a bomber," he fired at Cash and Skyler, who were deep in discussion at the mouth of the hallway. "If you could possibly believe she is, Cash Dixon, you are not the man I thought you were."

Skyler shook her head and went down the hall with Veronica. Cash opened his mouth to speak, then clamped it closed and started searching the family room. Tears at his continued belief in her guilt stung Krista's eyes. She angrily swiped them away. Not anger at Cash, but anger at the situation. Maybe at God for allowing it and at herself for foolishly thinking she could rely on Cash.

"Don't cry, Liebchen," Opa said softly. "Everything will be okay."

He continued offering words of encouragement, but she didn't believe him. Couldn't believe him. Not after what had happened with Toby.

And worse yet, although she knew pigs would fly before Cash would sit next to her, hold her hand, support her and come to her defense, she wanted him there. By her side. Defending her as he'd pretty much done since this all started.

"Let's pray, Liebchen," Opa offered.

Krista didn't have the heart to say no, so she joined him by bowing her head. She listened to his heartfelt plea. Admired his complete trust in God. Felt herself wondering if this was just another of those situations where God was trying to get her attention.

Well, God, she prayed, *if You're trying to tell me something, I'm not seeing it so please make it clearer.*

Krista heard footsteps coming down the hallway. She opened her eyes.

Skyler poked her head into the room. Her focus went straight to Cash. "You'll want to see this."

"Stay there," he said to Krista as he passed her.

She started to rise.

Opa held her down. "Do as they ask or things will only get worse."

She could hardly sit still with fears running through her brain. Had the bomber planted something else? Made her look even guiltier? If so, was it time to get out of town?

She didn't want to leave Opa, but if she was arrested, she wouldn't be able to help him and his worry would hamper his recovery. Better she grab her bag and go. Once she reached her destination, she could call him to tell him she was safe. Then he could relax and heal.

She heard Skyler's and Cash's footsteps heading toward them. She held her breath, her heart pounding wildly. Her palms grew moist. She scrubbed them down her pant legs.

Cash came first, his expression rock hard and cold. Krista didn't have to wonder if the news was bad. His icy look made it all clear. She was in trouble here. Big trouble. Perhaps she'd even waited too long to depart, and the man she was starting to have feelings for was going to slap handcuffs on her wrists and arrest her.

Outside the interrogation room at County, Cash stood next to Brady and looked through the observation window. Few places other than jail or prison were more unwelcoming than the small, airless box where detectives interrogated suspects. Cold cinder-block walls. A metal table with slots for handcuffs to restrain suspects. Hard metal chairs. No window.

A room where Krista didn't belong. At least that's what Cash's heart was telling him, but his brain was trying to send a far different message.

After their discovery of her bag in the crawl space, Skyler had brought Krista in hoping to get answers to questions she'd sidestepped at home.

No charges had been filed, but Krista wasn't free to leave until Skyler gave her approval.

Despite Krista's ongoing evasiveness, he'd wanted to help her but he couldn't do anything when she refused to confide in him. Instead, he watched as Skyler settled Krista in the same seat Otto had held moments ago. Skyler started grilling Krista, who responded in a weak voice that played over the speaker above. Skyler continued to toss out questions, but Krista offered very little in defense. Not even when Skyler set the bag from the crawl space on the table and pulled the items out one at a time. A large stack of cash. A passport with Krista's picture. Driver's license. Credit cards. All of them in Leah James's name.

Had Krista fooled Cash? Was he a chump for believing in her when the evidence of her deception was growing by the day? Was Brady right that Cash was letting a very cagey woman pull the wool over his eyes? A woman who possessed everything she needed to run far away from all of them. From him.

Maybe, but her pain right now was real. The tears rolling down her cheeks were real, too. So was the way her arms wrapped around her body in defense. She hadn't done any of this. She might be responsible for the fake ID they'd discovered, but he couldn't shake the feeling that the detonator had been planted.

Not that he'd told Krista how he felt. He'd been

so unfeeling at the house, and he wanted to take it back. To storm into the room and tell Skyler to take it easy. To hold Krista and promise he'd make everything all right. To keep on holding her.

"Take a few minutes to think about this, Ms. Curry." Skyler came to her feet and planted her hands on the table. "I'd hate to hold you here until you decide to talk, but I will." After a long pointed look at Krista, Skyler stepped from the room.

Krista put her hands over her face and sagged in the chair. Her shoulders shook, and Cash knew she was finally letting go of the emotions she'd tried so hard to hold in check.

The door opened, and Skyler joined them. She wore a frustrated scowl. "I don't get her. Despite the detonator, I really don't see Ms. Curry being involved in this mess. If she'd just tell us the truth about why she has a fake ID, we could check out her story, and I could let her go."

"You won't get anything out of her," Brady said. "She's a tough one to crack."

"Then I'll have to hold her until she talks."

"Isn't that reaching?" Cash asked. "I get that we found the detonator, but there's no link to the actual bomb. It didn't even have her fingerprints on it. Plus, there were no traces of explosives found in the house or on the detonator. And the bag only proves she has a false ID. We still have no motive or reason for her to blow up the stadium and no trace of a connection to the staff or vendors to sneak it in past security."

"I can hold her for the forged ID alone."

"But you won't, right?" Cash asked. "You're frustrated with her, but keeping her in lockup won't make her talk."

Skyler crossed her arms. "She's a flight risk."

"I'm sure she'll agree to leave the items in the bag in your custody, and I'll be with her 24/7 so she can't go anywhere."

"You're still going to babysit her?" Brady carefully watched Cash.

"Nothing has changed. She and Otto are still in danger. I won't leave them on their own."

"Tell you what," Brady said. "Why don't I take the next shift on her protection detail?"

Cash's gut revolted at the idea. "No! Absolutely not."

Brady and Skyler exchanged a knowing look. Cash didn't care. He was too busy thinking about his own adamant refusal. His reaction said Krista had gotten to him more than he'd suspected.

What an idiot. Falling for a suspect. *She has a fake ID, for crying out loud.*

What part of not letting someone into his life when he was still a mess over losing the team was he not getting? Was bad enough that he was an idiot for letting Krista in, but worse yet, he no longer knew if he could trust his judgment when it came to her. He needed to step this interest in her down a notch, but he still wouldn't leave her in danger.

"Okay," he said. "So maybe I've got a thing for her, but—"

Brady snorted, interrupting him.

He looked at Skyler. "But I won't let that stand in the way of making sure nothing bad happens to her or Otto. In fact, we can use it to our advantage. Release her into my custody, and I'll keep trying to get an answer about the bag."

Skyler frowned. "I don't know."

"He has a point," Brady offered, surprising Cash. "If anyone can get her to talk, it'll be Cash. If he doesn't, you can always take her back into custody."

Skyler eyed Cash for a long moment. "Okay, but you're to stick to her like glue. Got it?"

Despite cautioning himself mere moments ago, the thought of being that close to Krista made him smile.

"Let me give her a stern warning about not attempting to leave your custody. Then she's all yours," Skyler said before departing.

Cash watched as Krista's head shot up at the news of her pending freedom. He saw her blow out a long breath and sit up taller. Skyler issued her warning.

"I won't go anywhere," Krista declared. "I promise."

"Then you're free to go."

Krista rushed toward the door.

"One more thing, Ms. Curry." Skyler stepped in front of Krista. Skyler pulled her shoulders back while planting her feet in a way that made her seem six feet tall and always got people's attention. "Cash is a fine man and a well-respected member of our team. Don't use the fact that he believes in you to cause him any harm. Our team wouldn't look too fondly on that kind of behavior."

"You have nothing to worry about. I respect him, too, and appreciate his kind consideration for my grandfather and me."

"Then we'll have no problem." Skyler stepped aside.

Cash hated that Skyler felt a need to issue the warning, but he didn't mind hearing Krista's response and seeing that she wasn't too angry with him after he'd been so rough on her at the house. He went to meet her at the doorway, and they picked up Otto on the way out. Cash escorted them to the car.

"So what happens now?" Krista asked after they'd buckled their seat belts. "With the investigation, I mean. Does Skyler think I'm the bomber? Has she given up on looking for the real guy now?"

"No, of course not."

"But she thinks I'm involved, doesn't she?"

"I'm not at liberty to discuss that."

"Okay, can you discuss any other leads she might have mentioned?"

"She did say back at the house that she's releasing the bomber's sketch to the media in hopes that someone recognizes him."

Krista shot Cash a terrified look. "They won't release my name in conjunction with that, right?"

He shook his head. "We can't stop the press from speculating, but our team would never reveal any information about you."

She watched him carefully, her looked filled with skepticism.

"What?" he asked. "You don't believe me?"

She shrugged. "It's all just so unsettling, I don't know what or who to believe anymore."

Cash could totally relate to that sentiment. He didn't know what to believe, either, but unlike her, he couldn't let it get in the way of his job. If he did, someone could die.

Cash stood gazing out into the night, his hands shoved into his pockets. Krista wanted to peek at his expression but remained seated on the sofa. Since the discovery of the detonator, a wall of silence had gone up between them. He knew she was withholding something, and her failure to confide in him had clearly disappointed him. Bigtime. She wanted to tell him about her past, but for all she knew, Skyler was counting on Krista's guard being down with Cash and her revealing information to him.

Which meant she needed to be even more on guard around him. How was she supposed to do that when he was doing the right thing here? Standing guard. Caring for her and Opa. Following through on his commitment. Everything she hoped for in a man.

He turned and caught her watching him. "You look like you have something to say."

Did she? Maybe.

She got up. Crossed over to him. "I don't want you to think I'm not grateful for your help." She smiled sincerely and met his gaze. "This is all so overwhelming. Terrifying, actually, but you… Without you…it would… I—" Stress from the past few days stole her words. Tears pricked her eyes. She tried to blink them back and looked away from his compassionate gaze to get control of her emotions.

"Hey, hey," he soothed. "Don't you know guys can't handle it when a woman cries?" He quirked a smile.

She tried to return it, but her mouth trembled.

"Aw, c'mon, Krista. Don't cry." He brushed tears away from her cheek, his touch an instant comfort. "I can't stand to see you so upset."

He dropped his hand to hers and drew her closer. His eyes riveted to hers. The depth of his concern and caring was unmasked and she could hardly breathe. Her eyes locked on his. She was drawn toward him. Step by step. He lowered his head. His lips descended toward hers. She clutched his shoulder and lifted up on her toes. Prepared herself for the touch of his lips. Something she'd wanted for days, if she was honest about it.

"Liebchen…" Opa's voice came down the hallway. "Could you help me with… Oh, I am interrupting."

She jerked away from Cash. Took a deep breath. "No, you're not. What did you need?"

"An extra blanket, but I can't reach the top shelf."

"I'll get it." She all but ran from the room, charging past a surprised Opa.

She pulled down the fuzzy blanket and hugged it to her chest.

How could she have almost kissed Cash? They were so unsuitable for each other. Both with their own secrets. Both vulnerable and hurting.

She had to watch herself around him. She couldn't ever forget her poor judgment in men. She'd find herself in a world of hurt again. If that wasn't enough reason, these developing feelings for Cash could distract her at a time when clearing her name was more important than ever before.

SIXTEEN

Cash watched Krista leave the room, his mouth hanging open in surprise. Not for the way she'd bolted, but for his reaction to her. He'd almost kissed her. Dumbest of all moves he could make. A part of him hated himself for wanting to kiss her when he still couldn't believe in her innocence. What kind of man did that make him?

Otto sat on the sofa and patted the seat next to him. "Come sit by me, Cash."

His mind still reeling, Cash reluctantly joined Otto.

"These feelings you have for my Krista," Otto said. "Are they serious?"

"What?" Cash's focus transferred to Otto. "That's the last thing I expected you to want to talk about."

Otto's eyes narrowed in a way Cash hadn't seen before, upping Cash's concern.

"She has been hurt in the past." Otto met and held Cash's gaze. "Badly. I need to know your intentions are honorable."

"Intentions." Cash jumped to his feet. *Intentions?* "I don't think I *have* any intentions."

"That makes me sad. This is the first time in years that Krista has seemed so interested in a man. I'd hoped when this investigation was over that you two might have something together." As Otto studied him, Cash felt as if the man could see clear through him. "I think you are the right man for her."

So much for Otto seeing him well. He was the last man she should risk getting involved with, and he respected Otto too much to let him think otherwise. "I'm not really relationship material right now, Otto." Cash gave a CliffsNotes version of losing his teammates. "I can't seem to shake it, you know? I've tried everything, but I can't find my way in the world again."

"The answer is simple, my friend. It is not to try harder on your own but to rely on God to get you through this."

Cash was disappointed. He'd hoped Otto actually had an answer. *The* answer Cash hadn't found. "I tried the faith thing, Otto. Failed bigtime. If I could just get a handle on why God let something like this happen, then maybe I could move on."

"He does not require us to know why things happen. Just to let Him take control of our lives and trust that He has our best interest at heart."

"And that's the problem." Cash dropped back

onto the sofa. "I keep waiting for the next big ca-
tastrophe to take me down again, and honestly…"
He paused to run a hand over the taut muscles in
his neck. "I'm on edge most of the time."

Otto patted Cash's knee. "Ah, see, that is where
you are going wrong, son. Living a trouble-free
life is impossible. Do not waste time or effort
striving for that. It is finding peace in the trouble
that you should strive for."

Peace, Cash thought. The very thing he was
missing in his life. He looked at the old man in
wonder. He had stage three cancer, plus this turmoil surrounding Krista, and Cash had never seen
Otto lose his peace. "You certainly set a good example. Always in such good spirits."

"Because I trust God to walk with me and take
me through the trouble to the other side. That is
where you can see your strength." Otto poked
Cash's chest. "I see that strength in you right now."

Cash snorted. "Not sure you're looking at the
right guy here."

"I am, son. Remember, no one perfects this. We
all fall back into old habits at times. Do not let this
uncertainty control your life. Let go. Trust God."

"Makes a lot of sense."

"Of course it does. I am a wise old man." Otto
chuckled.

"Trying to pull the wool over Cash's eyes, I
see," Krista said, entering the room. "I put the
blanket on your bed, and I'm turning in."

"I'll walk with you." Otto got up. "Remember, Cash. I see your strength. You can see it, too."

"Good night, Otto, and thanks." Cash felt Krista's curious gaze light on him, but he didn't turn to look. Soon he heard their footsteps heading down the hallway.

He grabbed the sheet and started making up the couch. He'd all but given up on working this problem out in his life, but Otto had given him something to think about. Maybe God could help Cash beat this thing and find the elusive peace. He settled into his makeshift bed and slept better than he had in a while. He woke with renewed optimism and even whistled as he showered, dressed and then folded his bedding.

"Someone is cheerful this morning." Otto stepped into the family room with Krista.

"I'm trying to channel you, Otto." Cash winked.

Krista nodded at the table. "What's in that coffee Opa gave you?"

"This is my secret, Liebchen." Otto chuckled.

Cash didn't let the good mood distract him from keeping a vigilant watch during the drive to Erwin's house to drop Otto off or on the way to the school. Despite needing to take care, he found himself smiling most of the morning. But when the News Channel Four van and Paul Parsons pulled up to the school building, unease took his smile.

Please let this be nothing, Cash prayed as he

went to meet Parsons. The sun had given way to clouds and a steady drizzle, perfect weather to have a talk with Parsons. He started to open his door, but Cash stopped him. Parsons lowered the window.

Cash lifted the collar of his jacket for warmth. "What can we do for you, Parsons?"

"I'm not here to see you. I want to talk to—"

"Krista's with her class right now," Cash interrupted. "And there's no way you'll get past me to talk to her."

Parsons narrowed his eyes. "I'll just come back later. Or stop by her house."

Cash widened his stance. "I'll be there then, too."

"Why not ask *him* about it?" the van driver suggested. "See what he thinks."

Parsons's eyes lit up. "A deputy's perspective on the latest development. I like it."

"No comment."

"I didn't even ask you anything."

"No comment," Cash said again, this time firing a stern glare at Parsons.

"So I guess that means you're okay with the fact that your primary witness to the bombing is wanted for murder."

"What?"

"Oh, wow." Parsons grinned. "You didn't know. This is priceless." Parsons swung his gaze to the driver. "Roll film."

"You do that and you'll be pulling that camera from out of your throat."

"Fine," Parsons said. "But you do want to know what I'm talking about, right?"

"Go ahead." Cash's words were as close as he would come to asking this guy for anything.

Parsons looked far too eager to tell his story for Cash's liking. "The night of the bombing something seemed familiar to me about Ms. Curry. I rarely forget a face so I did a little digging. Took me a while to track it down, but I finally figured it out and found all I need to know about her from our archives." He paused and his eyes lit up. "Her real name is Krista Alger. Married to a Toby Alger, who wound up dead after committing one of the biggest senior scams in the country. Portland Police Bureau detectives discovered a half-million dollars in her joint account with hubby had gone missing. They could never prove she killed her husband or took the money, but the money's never been recovered, and her name was never cleared of the missing money or her hubby's death."

Cash's peace evaporated in a flash and he took a stunned step back. Krista was suspected of killing her husband. That was bad. Really bad, but worse yet, she hadn't told Cash about it. He thought they'd reached a point where she would share something this major with him, but she hadn't.

Realization dawned, and he took another step

back, his mind reeling. This was her secret. *The* secret. The big one that she wouldn't tell anyone. And boy howdy, he could see why she wouldn't. If she had been involved in scamming seniors, she could have criminal connections that would make her involvement with the bomber seem less outrageous.

Question was, what else was she hiding?

Cash spotted the PPB detective investigating Toby Alger's death the minute he stepped in the coffee shop door for their meeting. Cops just had that look about them that you could peg a mile away, and Detective Eason was no exception. As Eason lowered his stout body into a chair, Cash made quick work of introductions. This conversation couldn't wait, but the sooner he could push through it, the sooner he could get back to the school and relieve Brady, who was standing watch over Krista.

"Tell me about the investigation," Cash said. "Specifically Krista Cu—Alger's role in it."

Eason took a long sip of his coffee, then rested his elbows on the table. "One morning Toby Alger doesn't wake up. Wife calls it in. At first, it looked like he died from natural causes. The ME suspected a heart attack, but then she gets Alger's tox screen back." He paused as if hoping to create drama.

"And?" Cash pushed him along.

"And she finds GHB and Valium in his system. The cause of death, actually. The combination suppressed his breathing. He had a prescription for the Valium, but the wife claims she didn't know he was taking it."

"Seems odd," Cash said. "A wife usually knows about any drugs her husband is taking."

"Our thoughts exactly," Eason said and leaned back. "Of course, she claims not to know about the GHB, either. We begin to think she might've poisoned her husband, so we start digging for motive. We discover Alger masterminded a cleverly disguised Ponzi scheme. He'd scammed hard-earned savings from the elderly, leaving many of them penniless."

Cash tried to imagine Krista with a man who'd bilk seniors and couldn't reconcile that vision with the woman he was coming to know. Of course, he didn't know everything about her, now, did he?

"What was Krista's role in all of this?" Cash dreaded the answer but forced himself to keep his focus on Eason.

"Wait until you hear this," Eason said excitedly. "We found Alger's bank statement for a joint account that once held half a mil, but the money was moved electronically just two days before Alger's death." Eason draped an arm across a chair. "And that, my friend, is what we homicide detectives call a red flag. A big honkin' red flag."

Cash wasn't going to encourage Eason's obvious arrogance with a comment. "Did you figure out where the money went?"

"Nope, and not for lack of trying. The electronic transmission originated at the Alger house."

"And you think Krista moved it? Why not Alger himself?"

"Makes sense that she did it. Then hubby found out and demanded it back. Maybe threatened to kill her, so she took care of him before he did her in."

Cash could barely stomach the thought. "What about an alibi? Did Krista have one?"

"She was at home at his time of death so no alibi there."

"Doesn't mean she poisoned him. He could've gotten the drug anywhere and come home before it kicked in."

"You're right. We never did find out how he ingested the drugs."

"What about an alibi for when the money transfer occurred?"

"She has a witness who places her at the movies at that time."

"But you don't buy it?"

Eason shrugged.

"Why not?"

"For that kind of money, she could easily have given someone a key to her house to make the transfer while she sat at the theater. Maybe pay the same person to score the drugs to kill the husband."

Or she'd been exactly where she'd said—at the theater. "Did you find any evidence of that or any other suspects at all?"

"Of course, we had the whole group of people Alger scammed, who had motive to kill him. Not that a group of seniors is real likely to commit murder or even know about GHB, but still, we worked the list. Investigated them and their children, leaving no stone unturned. You know, in case the kid's expecting to inherit a wad from the parents or they're just upset their parents had been scammed out of hard-earned money. Maybe leaving their parents' care up to them now."

"And?"

"Found a couple of possibilities, but we never really located anyone with means and opportunity. So the wife continued to sit at the top of our list. Didn't help that she took off." He frowned. "We had nothing to hold her on, but she just ups and disappears. Now we find out she's been living under an assumed name. The one she used while on the run with her killer daddy. Makes her look guilty in my book."

"Wait, what are you talking about with this killer-daddy thing?" Cash tried to hold the surprise from his tone but didn't manage it.

"Oh, you didn't know, huh?" Eason picked up his cup again and sipped. "Her father ran a chop shop. His partner tries to squeeze him out, and he kills the partner. We question the dad. He takes off. She goes with dear old dad and they skate under the radar in Georgia for quite a few years until the guy's father-in-law rats him out. Probably where the daughter learned her disappearing skills. Like father, like daughter." He smirked.

Cash wanted to wipe the look off Eason's face.

Eason set down his cup. "Put all that together, and in my book, it says guilty."

Not in Cash's book. Evidence and evidence alone declared someone's guilt.

Evidence like a detonator, his mind warned him. Was he listening to his heart again?

Not regarding the missing money and Toby Alger's murder. Eason clearly had no solid evidence. Without it, it was a detective's job to keep an open mind. If this guy had treated Krista the way Cash suspected he had, no wonder she ran.

"So she remains the only suspect?" Cash asked, hoping to wind up this conversation and talk to Krista about it.

"Actually, we have another lead, but that's not something I'm willing to discuss. This is still an ongoing investigation. We don't want anything leaked."

"I'm not planning on sharing it."

"Sorry, man." Eason crossed his arms. "It's on a need-to-know basis. Without an official request, my LT would kill me for disclosing it. Besides, it'll likely lead back to Krista Alger anyway. With this bombing, she's proving her criminal intents."

Cash hated how blatantly this guy wanted to nail Krista at all costs. Cash stood. "You'll be getting that official request from Deputy Skyler Brennan. She's lead on our investigation."

"Be glad to cooperate if she goes through proper channels."

She would follow protocol, all right. Cash would make sure of that. He dialed her number the minute he stepped outside and recounted Eason's conversation for her. Silence stretched out between them.

"Look," Cash said to break the quiet, "I know what you're thinking. Krista's been involved in the criminal world since she was young. Even lived with a father who was on the run. But that doesn't make her a killer. Or a bomber, for that matter."

"That's not what I was thinking."

"Then what?" Cash asked as he crossed to his car.

"I was wondering when you called earlier to tell me about Parsons's claim, why you didn't mention that you were planning on talking to the detective."

"Is that a problem?"

"We work as a team, Cash, and that's not teamwork."

He dropped onto the cold seat and tried not to get mad at the lecture. "Okay, I get it. I wasn't trying to leave you out of it. I just reacted."

"Reacting as you've been doing all along. It's

not solid police work." She sighed. "We've all gotten accustomed to having your ugly mug around, and I'd hate to see you lose your job over a woman who may have a prison stint in her future."

Anger fired in Cash's gut, and he shoved his free hand into his hair. "That won't happen. For her or me. Not if you request that report.

"Okay, okay," she said. "No need to get testy. I'll get the official request in the works when we hang up."

"You'll call me the minute you get the information from Eason?"

"If it's sensitive like the detective claims, you know I can't share it with you."

"Of course you can."

She sighed. "You have no official role in her husband's murder investigation, Cash. Even as the lead investigator on the stadium investigation, they won't want to share Alger's details. I'll have to work hard to make them see the possible connection to my case."

His anger burned out of control. "Of all the lame things."

"Not lame. We can't do anything to jeopardize their murder investigation."

"Fine," Cash barked into phone. "I'll figure this out on my own."

"Don't let your involvement with Krista make you do something stupid."

Stupid? He'd already done something stupid.

SEVENTEEN

Krista had thought about having lunch with Cash all morning, but his expression stopped her cold. He didn't look mad. More upset. She was afraid to ask about what had happened to his good mood, but she was also afraid not to.

She grabbed the lunch Opa had packed from the lounge refrigerator and joined Cash at the table. "Looks like something's bothering you."

He met her gaze squarely. "So do I call you Krista Curry or Krista Alger? Or even Leah James? Or is there another name you've gone by that I should know about?"

No. Oh, no. It had happened. He'd learned her secret.

He shook his head, his distrust obvious. "It also would've been nice if you'd mentioned that you were suspected of murder."

Murder. The word whispered through her head and stole her breath. She dropped to the chair across from him.

"Why didn't you tell me, Krista?" he asked, his gaze riveted to her.

"I wanted to, but…"

"But what?"

"You wouldn't understand."

"Try me."

She couldn't talk about it. Not yet. "How'd you find out?"

"Paul Parsons stopped by this morning."

"The reporter," she muttered as sad resignation hit. Her life was about to take an even bigger turn for the worse. "It's going to start all over again, isn't it? The stories. The accusations. The looks and finger-pointing." She shook her head. "Poor Opa. He doesn't deserve to deal with this again."

"I'd like you to tell me what happened." His voice was less harsh but still skeptical.

"You already know." She stared at her hands to keep from seeing the look of disgust on his face when she confirmed the details.

"I'm trying my best not to form an opinion here, but you're making it hard for me not to believe the worst."

She looked up at him and tears threatened to fall. She blinked hard. She wouldn't cry. Not now. Later tonight. When she was alone. Maybe when Cash was gone from their lives and was no longer protecting her and Opa.

No. No, she couldn't let that happen. Not when the bomber was still out there. Not when he was still trying to terrorize her and when Opa could potentially be attacked again. She had to do her best to convince Cash to stay with them. To convince him of her innocence.

That meant sharing her side of Toby's investigation. She thought back to the beginning. The morning she woke up next to Toby. "I thought Toby had turned off the alarm and gone back to sleep," she said, the memory still as real today as four years ago. "But he was cold. His lips were purple. I checked his pulse. It was…oh, man…the moment I realized. It was horrible. So horrible."

Her voice caught in her throat and tears flooded her eyes. She didn't want to go on, but somehow she managed to start again. "I called 911. They thought he'd had a heart attack and took him away. Opa and I started making funeral arrangements. Then the detectives showed up on my doorstep." The memory of their harsh treatment gave rise to her anger and helped slow her tears. "They said he'd been drugged. That he was a scammer and stole money from seniors. I was shocked. But it got worse. They claimed I'd moved the money."

"*Did* you move the money? Or kill him?"

She gaped at his questions.

"I have to hear you say it, Krista."

"No. No. No!" she shouted, then lowered her voice before it carried to the children in the back of the building. "I did not kill my husband. I did not steal the money. The only thing I did wrong was trust a man who had secrets. And I've paid for it for the last four years. Being run out of my home. Forced to leave Opa behind."

Cash watched her and she knew he was looking to see if she was telling the truth. "You didn't know anything about this money, either, right? Your clothes are designer. I'd say you live a good life."

She thought to deny it but she imagined his loathing at her response and she couldn't speak. She stared out the window, watching the rain pick up and cloud the glass as her life was now clouded with additional turmoil.

"No answer? Why?" he demanded.

"I don't want to see your disgust," she replied quietly, but made eye contact.

Disappointment crowned on his face. "So you did know, then?"

"No, I didn't know about the scam. And I certainly didn't know about the half a million—I had no idea there was ever that much in our account. No…it's just… Toby was a financial analyst so he took care of our finances. I'll admit to wondering at times if he was bringing home more money than he should."

"But you didn't ask."

She shook her head. "I should have, but after living with my father in near poverty conditions, I liked the things the money bought. I'm not proud of it, but I liked the nice house. Nice

clothes. Fancy car. If I'd asked Toby, maybe…"
She ended with a shrug.

"You thought it might all go away."

"Yes," she said, then let out a hoarse laugh. "It went away anyway after Toby died and the police froze all of our assets. Then when they freed up the money, lawsuits from the people he swindled took everything but the clothes on my back. I'm still wearing them four years later because my minimum-wage job means I can't afford to buy more. But I don't care about that. I really don't. It was the hatchet job the reporters did on me and the cruelty of people that really hurt. Breaking into my house. Spray-painting messages of hate on the walls. I had to leave town. For mine and Opa's sake."

"Is that when you took back the Curry name?"
She nodded.

He looked at her for a long time, searching for something. "Your credentials are impeccable. Not something the average person can obtain."

She cringed.

"Something else you're not telling me?"

She felt as if she might throw up and didn't want to talk about this, but if she wanted Cash's assistance, she needed to be completely forthright. She clutched her hands in her lap, squeezing to keep her mind focused. "My father. He's in prison for murder."

To Cash's credit he didn't show any surprise. "Tell me about him."

She took a moment to gather her thoughts, then started her story. "As far as I was concerned, he ran a legitimate auto repair shop, nothing more. Then when I was sixteen, Opa heard my dad had killed a man. Something to do with stolen car parts. Opa believed the stories and reported them to the police. They questioned Dad and he was afraid they would arrest him. I didn't believe Opa. As my only parent after Mom died, maybe I just didn't want to see that he was guilty." Memories of the tumultuous time in her teenage life came rushing back and she fell silent.

"So what happened?"

"Dad decided to take off, and I asked to go with him. We didn't tell Opa where we went. That was the hardest part. Dad bought fake IDs and we moved to Kennesaw. We kept our first names to simplify things, but Dad didn't want me dragged into his mess if his cover was ever blown so he insisted on a different last name."

"That's why his name was Nealy and yours Curry."

She nodded. "We settled into our life. Dad worked as a mechanic. In addition to going to school, I worked part-time as an aide in a home child-care center to make ends meet. But I missed Opa something fierce. So when it was time to graduate from high school, I invited him to the ceremony. He showed up with evidence the police had collected, proving my dad's guilt. I was in shock. Still am, I guess. He'd really killed a man. We had no choice. We had to turn him in."

"That must have been rough."

"Rough?" She wrapped her arms around her stomach. "There isn't a word to describe how it felt."

"And this is when you came back to live with Otto?"

"Yes. I took back my real last name of Fischer. Opa had my diploma switched to that name. I got my teaching degree, taught third grade and met and married Toby. After he died, I went back to Georgia. I couldn't use my degree and I knew I could easily get a job at the same in-home childcare center where I worked in high school. Then I took the preschool position here because that didn't require a degree, either. The rest you know."

"How long were you and Toby married?"

"Three years." She looked Cash square in the eye. "I didn't know what he was up to. And I had nothing to do with his death. You have to believe me."

"I want to." He settled his hand over hers, but his eyes remained skeptical. "I do. But do you know how bad this looks? It adds to the questions the team already has about you."

She jerked back, but he didn't release her hand. "They know already?"

"Just Skyler. She's lead investigator. I had to tell her." He squeezed her hand. "I'm trying not to let her opinion color my judgment."

Krista thought about the men and women of the FRS she'd come to care for and how they would react the way she'd expected. It hurt that they didn't trust her. That Cash couldn't believe her. But he was trying. That was enough for now. It was more than anyone other than Opa had ever given her. She was thankful for even that little bit. Still, she could no longer hold her tears back. Big fat ones plopped onto the table, and deep sobs wrenched free.

"Hey." Cash slid closer. "Hey."

"S-s-sorry."

"Oh, man." He went around the table and drew her into his arms.

She went willingly and rested against the solid wall of his chest. Felt his heart beat. Felt the depth of her feelings for this big, tough guy who was holding her so tenderly. She remained in his arms, his care and consideration slowing her tears.

She leaned back. Peered into his eyes filled with emotions. He lowered his head and she knew he was going to kiss her. She didn't care that she was at work. The room was private, the door closed, everyone else in the classrooms. She rose up. He settled his lips on hers. It was a demanding kiss as if he had to prove something. Maybe to himself. Maybe to her. She didn't know. But then it gentled and deepened.

She wanted this. Wanted him. But all her old insecurities came flooding back.

She pulled back and looked up at him. At this man who'd been by her side through all of this. She considered his many wonderful qualities. The ones Opa kept harping about.

But he's the same man who'd just told Skyler about your past, about the detonator.

She wanted to trust him. But she couldn't. Not with her heart. Not yet.

At the end of the school day, Cash escorted Krista down the hallway in silence, not sure what to think about today's events. He'd started the day with such high hopes. With the peace of God in his life. Then he'd found out about Krista's past and it evaporated. One bit of bad news and he let that peace disappear. If he couldn't control his mood swings for even a day, what was the likelihood he could master them at all?

They reached the hallway leading to the parking lot. Sounds of a loud commotion filtered down the hallway.

He turned to Krista. "Is the school holding an event?"

"No," she said, sounding uneasy.

"Wait here while I check it out." He went to the front door and found a slew of reporters standing at the ready, Parsons the first in line. Obviously, he'd leaked the story about Krista's past and other media outlets had picked it up. Cash wished Krista didn't have to deal with this, but the only way to his car was through this mob.

He returned to her. "Reporters are waiting for you. Just keep your head down, stay behind me, and I'll clear a path for us."

"Okay," she said uncertainly.

"I'll get you through this." He squeezed her hand. "I promise."

She didn't seem to believe him, but she nodded and pulled her raincoat tighter. He led the way to the door. The reporters descended like vultures. Cash ignored them and the cold, spitting rain and took off, checking to be sure Krista was behind him. She'd taken only a few steps before a tall blond reporter blocked Krista's path.

"Is it true that your real name is Krista Alger?" the reporter asked. "And you've been implicated in the bombing in addition to being an ongoing suspect in your husband's murder?"

Krista planted her feet and threw her shoulders back. She looked fierce and strong. Capable. She might be ignoring his directions, but he was proud of her strength and tenacity.

"I am not implicated in anything, and I did not kill my husband." The force in her tone didn't surprise Cash. She was a strong woman who had faced each day for years despite trouble hanging over her head.

Parsons pushed past the reporter and put his microphone in Krista's face. "Our source tells us that a detonator like one used to make a bomb was found in your home."

Krista's confidence crumbled.

Parsons smirked. "I take it from your reaction that it's true."

"Enough." Cash stepped in. "Ms. Cu—Alger has no more time for questions."

Instead of starting for the car, Krista spun and went back inside.

Cash followed her. "What are you doing?"

She swiped wet hair from her face, looking angry and determined. "I'm resigning and cleaning out my things."

"What? Why?"

"This is just beginning. Now that they've found me, they'll turn into sharks again. Stalk me at all hours. Neighbors will grow tired of the media. Tired of a murderer and bomber in their neighborhood and will threaten me and Opa." Her voice rose with every word, sounding as if she was close to losing control. As fast as her temper flared, she calmed and her stony determination returned. "I may not be able to do anything for Opa short of leaving again, but I can prevent the church and the children from going through this." She marched toward the office.

Cash caught up to her. "Maybe you should wait. Just take a leave of absence."

She spun on him. "A leave? You think this is going to go away soon? Toby died four years ago, and I'm still living this nightmare. Opa's still living it."

He thought about his conversation with Otto last night. He could handle this. "Otto will be just fine. His faith will see him through it."

"You're right," she said, sounding sad. "But I'm not sure I can survive another round of utter and complete humiliation."

EIGHTEEN

Krista stepped out of Peggy's office and lifted the hood on her raincoat to keep her face off camera. She headed for the door, perhaps for the last time. Peggy had convinced Krista to take a leave of absence as Cash had suggested, but Krista doubted she'd be back.

She should be thankful for this latest development. Because one thing was now crystal clear. She couldn't do this anymore. The worry. The stress. The anxiety. She could finally admit that, despite her best efforts, her life had spiraled beyond her control and she needed help—God's help—to get out of it.

She met Cash at the exit. At the chaotic scene outside, her feet stuttered to a stop by the door. She looked at him. "I was so wrapped up in what was going on, I didn't think to ask how the press heard about the detonator. Did you tell them?"

He frowned. "No, of course not."

"Then how did they find out? Did someone else on the team leak it?"

"Not intentionally, I assure you, but I wondered

the same thing so I called Skyler. She didn't say anything to the press."

"What about the rest of your team?" Krista hated to think someone on the FRS leaked the news, but after her experience with Toby's investigation, it wasn't hard to believe.

"I trust these guys implicitly and doubt they'd let it slip, but Skyler is checking on it." Cash gestured at the door. "I'll go first. This time promise you'll put your head down and keep moving no matter what they say."

"I promise." She dug deep for added courage and tailed Cash. Comments and questions were thrown out. Words like *murderer* and *bomber* made her cringe. The name-calling didn't stop Cash. He barreled ahead. Though they weren't touching, she felt his presence and support.

He blocked the mob, helped her into the car and took off with a squeal of the tires. They headed to Erwin's house, and she looked at Cash to assess his mood. Regardless of the terrible things he'd just learned about her, he sat tall and strong. Her defender. Her protector.

How blessed she was to have met him. For his protection, sure, but he'd also brought so many feelings to the surface since she'd known him. Some good. Some bad. All things she needed to examine. Perhaps God had put him in her life to help her through this. Maybe He'd even put Cash there for her to realize that she could still feel something for a man. Still want love, marriage and a family. To help her see that she should let go of her fears and try believing in people again.

Her first step was to trust in her judgment to find the right kind of man. Not one like Toby. Or her father. Even Cash made her uneasy with his unwillingness to be straightforward with her.

She glanced out the window, surprised to see they'd arrived at Erwin's house.

Cash pulled into the driveway and cut the engine. "Would it be easier for you if I told Otto about the latest developments?"

"I'll tell him. I don't like what it's going to do to him, but in some respects, it feels good to have this all out in the open." She pulled her shoulders back in preparation. "I've had enough of keeping secrets and trying to hide things. I'm done with that."

Cash watched her for a moment, looking as if he wanted to say something. Instead, he stepped from the car. It felt as if he was still hiding something from her. Maybe he didn't know how to say it. Or more likely, he didn't trust her with the information. She didn't blame him.

At the door, he rang the bell and they stood in silence waiting. No one answered.

Cash stabbed the button again and knocked. Still no answer.

"Maybe they have the TV up too loud," Krista

said, though she didn't hear the TV. She tried the door. It swung open.

Cash scowled. "I warned them to keep this locked." He ran a finger over the doorjamb. "Looks like the lock's been jimmied. I'll check it out. You stay here." He drew his weapon and called Opa's name as he stepped into the entryway.

Thinking he was overreacting, Krista glanced inside. The entryway table lay on its side, a lamp smashed on the floor.

Had the bomber thought Opa possessed the item he was looking for? Broke in? Maybe hurt Opa?

Fear chilled Krista to the bone. She couldn't just stand here. She had to know if Opa was okay.

She crept inside. Slowly. Silently. Looking for clues along the way. She entered the family room. Cash squatted on the far side of the sofa. She couldn't see what he was looking at. She took a few more steps and got a clear view. She gasped.

Cash jumped to his feet and spun, his weapon trained on her. He mumbled something under his breath and lowered his gun. "What are you doing in here? I could have killed you."

"Is…is Erwin—"

"Alive?" Cash asked. "Yes, he's alive."

She stepped closer and gasped at the blood pooling around Erwin's head. She frantically looked around. Searching. Hoping.

"Where's Opa?" she cried out.

"I don't know. I haven't cleared the whole house yet. Go outside and call 911 while I check it out."

She didn't want to go. To leave Erwin alone and not search for Opa. But Cash was right. The intruder could still be there.

"Hurry!" she begged and offered a prayer for all of them on her way out the door.

She dialed 911, barely able to control her trembling fingers to tap the right numbers. She reported the situation and asked for an ambulance. As she was hanging up, Cash stepped outside. The pinched expression on his face sent her heart plummeting.

"Opa?" she asked.

"He's not here."

Panic took a deeper hold. She thought of Erwin lying on the floor. Hoping he'd regained consciousness and could tell her where to find Opa, she charged back inside. Cash called for her to stop, but she ignored him. She dropped to the floor by Erwin and cringed at the large gash to his head. Thankfully, it had stopped bleeding, but he remained unconscious.

She took a good look at the room. At furniture turned over. At a vase shattered in a million pieces. The pool of blood.

Panic threatened to take her down.

Cash knelt by her side, placed a comforting hand on her shoulder.

She peered at him. "There was a struggle. Do

you think…?" Unable to put voice to her concern, she let her words fall off.

"This was the work of the bomber and he took Opa?" Cash finished for her, his eyes somber and tortured. "Yes, that's exactly what I think."

Cash paced the floor in the firehouse family room, waiting for Skyler to arrive with evidence from Erwin's house. Krista sat on the edge of the sofa, the knees of her khaki pants caked with dried blood. She kept running her hands over the bloodstains and staring at her hands.

The front door opened and team members poured inside but no Skyler. Brady dropped onto the sofa next to Krista, his hands going for his pocketknife to whittle. Archer took one of the recliners, Jake the other.

Darcie sat next to Krista and held her hand. "I checked with the hospital. Erwin has a concussion, but he's awake and he's going to be fine."

"Thank You, God," Krista exclaimed.

Cash settled on the arm of the sofa. "Has anyone taken Erwin's statement?"

Jake shook his head. "He's still confused and putting things together. It might be some time before we get the details."

"I'm glad Erwin will be okay." Krista freed her hand and threaded her fingers together. "I couldn't stand the thought of someone getting hurt because of me."

"You're assuming this is due to the bombing," Archer said.

Krista shot him a look. "What else could it be?"

"A random home invasion."

"Odds are if it was a home invasion, they wouldn't have taken Otto," Cash argued. "Plus, there were valuables left behind."

"It's a waste of time speculating when we don't have the facts," Jake said. "Let's wait for Skyler's evaluation."

Everyone fell silent and tension mounted in the room. Cash wished he could do something to reduce it, but his go-to stress reliever was a joke, and he couldn't possibly joke with Otto missing.

Krista sat forward on the sofa, letting her focus travel around the group. Jake met her gaze, but Brady and Archer looked away from her.

"I suppose we should get the elephant in the room out of the way," she said. "I didn't murder my husband, no matter what the police and press claim."

A soft gasp escaped from Darcie's mouth, but Krista ignored it and launched into an explanation of Toby's death. Darcie appeared to buy Krista's story, but Cash's other teammates seemed skeptical. As they should be. As *Cash* should be, but he honestly believed in Krista. Something in his gut said she was the real deal and he hated seeing the doubt in his friends' eyes.

"I had nothing to do with Toby's fraud scheme or the money," Krista concluded and sat back.

Seeing questions lingering on Brady's face, Cash had to intervene before Brady could fire off one of his pointed questions.

"Krista's past isn't related to our bombing incident at all," Cash stated. "There's no point in discussing it further. Instead, we should focus on the bombing."

"And please know." Krista paused and smiled, but it was forced. "When Skyler's team finishes talking to the people with access to the stadium, you'll see that I have no connection to the bomber, either."

"Not true." Skyler stepped into the room and all heads turned in her direction. She held a plastic bag containing a cell phone and piece of paper. "You have a connection now. We found this phone and note under Erwin's body."

Cash couldn't abide her keeping them in dark like this. He grabbed the bag and flipped it over to get a good look at big bold letters on white paper.

"What does it say?" Krista asked, her face a mass of worry.

"He says—" Cash adjusted the note so he could see the entire page "—'I'll call tomorrow at 10:00 a.m. to arrange a trade. The item that belongs to me for your grandfather. Don't miss my call or the old man dies.'"

NINETEEN

"I don't have anything," Krista said, hoping to stop the FRS team from gawking at her. "If I did, I'd be pulling it out to save Opa. You have to believe that."

"She's right, you know." Cash returned to the arm of the sofa. "You have to agree that Krista wouldn't do anything to hurt Otto, right?"

The others nodded.

"Then there's no other choice but for us to believe she doesn't possess what the bomber is looking for. Otherwise, she'd hand it over right now."

"Another option is that it's not something she's aware of possessing," Skyler added.

"Maybe he means the detonator," Brady offered.

Skyler shook her head. "That's not worth abducting Otto to reclaim. We didn't lift any prints from it and there's no actual link to the bomb."

"At least this request confirms our theory that he's been looking for something," Cash offered.

"If I can't provide what he wants, he'll…" Krista couldn't say the words aloud.

"Why don't we grab some dinner?" Darcie suggested. "We've all had a long day and we'll think more clearly after something to eat."

She received mumbled agreements, but Krista's stomach was too upset to eat.

"It's my night to cook." Skyler stood. "If anyone wants to help, we could bang it out faster."

"I will." Krista jumped to her feet. "It'll keep my mind off Opa."

After a clipped nod, Skyler headed for the kitchen. She set a recipe for garlic lemon chicken with green beans and red potatoes on the counter. "If you could slice the lemons, I'll start on the potatoes." She put out a cutting board and retrieved the lemons and vegetables.

Krista took a knife from the block and started slicing while Skyler peeled potatoes.

"I owe you an apology." Skyler paused, her peeler in midair, as if she was thinking about how to continue.

Krista looked at her. "For what?"

"One of our new forensic techs told the press about the detonator." She met Krista's gaze head-on. "Rookies sometimes make mistakes. I assure you it won't happen again."

"I appreciate the apology, but the damage is done. Just like before."

"Before?"

"When Toby died, one of the detectives shared all the details—including his own speculations—

with the press. He made it seem like there was no doubt that I had killed Toby, even when they had no proof." Krista shook her head and went back to slicing, the tart lemon scenting the air.

"I suspect if he keeps that up, he won't be a detective for long."

Krista glanced at Skyler. "So it's not standard practice to leak details to make someone look guilty and make their life a living nightmare?"

"I don't see what purpose that would serve in the investigation. Certainly wouldn't help move it forward."

"I think he did it because he couldn't prove my guilt. He wanted me tried in the media to wear me down and make me confess."

Skyler's eyes narrowed as she seemed to think about it. "I suppose that could happen. Not something I'd condone, though. And it didn't work, did it?"

Krista shook her head. "I wouldn't confess to something I didn't do."

Skyler gave a quick nod and went back to her work. Maybe she was starting to believe in Krista's innocence. Maybe she'd always believed it and was just doing her job by keeping Krista on the suspect list. Krista would like to think so as she was starting to like Skyler.

They finished dinner prep in a comfortable silence. When they returned to the family room, the others looked up expectantly. Perhaps they thought Skyler had wormed some information out of Krista in the kitchen.

"Dinner's in an hour." Skyler sat and took out her phone.

Krista started to sit, too, but everyone continued to stare at her. The same way people had gaped at her when Toby's death filled the news. In stores. At work. In the neighborhood. Everyone, everywhere, their eyes filled with suspicion and blame. Everyone except Opa.

Opa, oh, Opa, where are you?

The walls felt as if they were closing in. She couldn't breathe. Think. She needed time alone. She spotted her raincoat on a hook and knew what would help relieve her stress. She crossed over to Cash. "Would it be okay if I stepped outside for a minute?"

"Sure," he said. "Let me turn on the garden light."

The light illuminated the steady rain soaking the patio. She grabbed her coat and slipped it on.

Cash opened the door for her. "I wouldn't mind the fresh air, too."

"I need to be alone."

He stepped back but caught her hand and squeezed it. "We'll figure this out and get Otto back. I promise."

"How can you promise that? No one can."

"You're right. I can only promise that I'll do everything within my power to get him back safely."

"Thank you." She smiled. "I could never have survived all of this without you." She stepped outside and the rain immediately wet her face. She tugged up her hood and stared over the garden. Wind whistled through tall ornamental grasses. Dark shadows clung to huge boulders holding back the earth in tiers.

She thought of Opa. Wondered where he was. If he was hurt. Hungry. Cold. She'd brought danger to his doorstep. Put his life on the line.

A sob tore from her throat. She swallowed it down as tears stung her eyes and blurred her vision.

She dug through her pockets for a tissue. She felt something hard. Something that had fallen through a hole between the pocket and lining of her coat. She worked the lining with her fingers until she freed the item.

Made of white plastic, it was the size of a credit card but thicker with a small raised section. She manipulated the compartment that seemed as if it should open, but it didn't budge. She'd never seen anything like it and had no idea how it ended up in her coat. Didn't belong to her, of that she was certain.

Maybe someone at school dropped it in the wrong jacket in the lounge. Or maybe it had to do with the bombing. Could it be what the bomber was looking for?

Excited by the possibility, she hurried inside,

went straight to Cash and showed him the card. "This was in my jacket pocket. With our dry spell, I left the coat in the teacher lounge. I haven't worn it since the morning after the bombing."

He took the card. "You think this has to do with the bombing?"

"Maybe. Or another teacher could've put it in my pocket by mistake. I don't know."

"Let's assume it's related to the bomb. How and when could it have ended up in your jacket?"

Krista closed her eyes and flashed back to that night. She hated the memories, but she let them play in her mind, reliving each little detail. Her eyes flew open. "The bomber pushed me out of the way. He could have dropped it into my pocket then." She grabbed Cash's arm. "He planted it on me and now he wants it back. This is it. Don't you see? The thing he's looking for. He couldn't find it when he searched the house because I'd left my jacket at school."

"But what is it?" Cash asked. "I've never seen anything like it."

"It's a credit card drive," Skyler said, coming into the room from the kitchen. She took the card and pressed the end of it. Up popped a tiny flash drive.

"Cool," Cash said. "But what's the point of it? Why not just carry a flash drive?"

"Flash drives can fall out of a pocket," Skyler said. "This tucks safely inside a wallet."

"If the bomber had this in his wallet," Brady commented, "it wouldn't have been easy to transfer it to Krista's pocket without her seeing him do it."

"Just because it fits in a wallet doesn't mean he had it there," Jake jumped in. "Might've been in his sweatshirt or pants pocket."

"We need to know what it contains." Cash looked at Skyler. "Can you grab your computer to open it?"

She shook her head. "Flash drives are notorious hack bombs. You put it in your computer and it kicks off a virus or runs malware. I won't take that risk with my computer. And, if this really is connected to the investigation, we need to follow evidence recovery protocol."

Krista frowned at her. "Which means what exactly?"

"We need to get a computer tech out here to image the drive and give us a copy of the files to look at."

"How long will that take?"

"Depends if the tech on call is dealing with something pressing." She dug out her phone. "I'll make a call and see."

As Skyler talked on the phone Krista could hardly stand still to wait for the news, but Skyler soon hung up. "He's on his way. We can have dinner while we wait."

"Eat?" Krista shouted. "How can anyone eat

when we might have the very thing the bomber is looking for to free Opa?"

After dinner, Cash wanted to force Skyler to move faster, but all he could do was stand behind the computer as it slowly opened the first file. The tech had taken the flash drive but had left them a copy of the files. The window opened to reveal a spreadsheet holding a long list of numbers and formulas.

Skyler scrolled down. "Any ideas on what we might be looking at here?"

"Don't ask me," Cash grumbled. "I never was a math wizard."

"Let me take a closer look." Archer changed places with Skyler. He clicked on a few of the cells to open long formulas far too complicated for Cash to figure out.

Archer shook his head and stood. "It's an algorithm of some sort, but I have no idea what for. We'll need to get someone with the right training to look at it."

"Okay, so why would the bomber give something like this to Krista?" Brady asked.

Krista scowled at him. Cash could tell she was getting tired of Brady always asking the hard question, but that was Brady through and through.

"Let's hold that thought until we look at the other files." Skyler clicked on the next item.

A schematic drawing opened.

"It's for a bomb." Cash leaned in to study the diagram and whistled. "It's more sophisticated than the stadium bomb. Open the other files."

Skyler clicked on them. They were all variations on the first diagram until she opened the last one.

"Whoa!" Brady pointed at it. "Is that what I think it is?"

Cash nodded. "A suicide vest with a handheld trigger remote. Question is, is it for the bomber or for someone else?"

"Terrorist?" Jake asked.

Krista paled. "What if he's going to make Opa wear it?"

Cash took her hand, not caring when the others stared at him. "He could be planning to use it as a security measure to make sure we hand over the right file."

Jake nodded. "If we screw it up…"

Krista gasped and dropped Cash's hand to clasp the back of a chair.

Cash glared at Jake. "Way to couch your words."

"Sorry," he said. "But it's a good possibility."

"Is it?" Cash asked. "He knows we have the plans and I can easily figure a way to disarm the device."

Brady scowled. "If he is planning to make Otto wear it, he could've switched things up to throw you off."

"Then we can't let that happen." Jake tapped

the screen. "What about these website addresses on this file? Can you trace him that way?"

Skyler shook her head. "There's no date or time he downloaded these diagrams. He could have done it years ago. It would be a needle in a haystack search."

"Okay." Jake leaned back. "So we have bomb schematics and a spreadsheet with algorithms. I don't see any reason this guy would off-load the drive on Krista." He looked around the group. "Anyone else?"

"A setup," Cash suggested. "After Krista told him about the backpack, he might have worried she would discover the bomb and report him. We'd question her involvement and find the card, making Krista look guilty.

"Or he was afraid it would implicate him," Archer said. "Think about it. Maybe he was afraid she'd report him before he got out of the stadium. He had no way of knowing the crowd would go wild, taking the attention of security officers. If he thought we'd detain him, the schematics would be enough to make him a suspect."

Cash nodded. "I'd buy that, but why not just throw it away? Why does he want this back? He could easily retrieve these schematics again."

Brady gestured at the computer. "Has to be the spreadsheet, then. Put this file in the right hands and we might be able to figure out the identity of our bomber."

Skyler closed the file. "I'll do my best to find an expert to review it tonight."

Jake clenched his jaw and worked the muscles. "We have until 10:00 a.m. tomorrow to figure that out, or Krista will have to make the exchange."

Cash saw Krista shrink back. "You can't really be thinking she should do the exchange? Especially not with these bomb schematics staring us in the face."

"We may not have a choice." Archer met Cash's gaze. "It's not a stretch to think this will be a non-negotiable point."

"Don't worry," Jake added. "We'll surround the area with a team to keep her safe and, of course, apprehend the bomber after the exchange."

The last thing Cash wanted was for Krista to go meet a bomber, but there was no point in saying anything tonight. "We can discuss it again once the bomber provides instructions."

"Okay, people." Jake clapped his hands. "We're done here. We'll reconvene in the morning at eight at the office."

The team dispersed, and Krista looked at Cash. "I should be getting home."

"What? Are you nuts?" His voice hit the ceiling. "You'll be spending the night here."

She shook her head. "I have to go home. The bomber might call the house or try to contact me there about Opa. Or even Opa could call. I plan to be there if he does."

TWENTY

Krista opened the coffee bean canister. The familiar aroma that had often comforted her in the past brought tears to her eyes tonight. Opa always ground the coffee before bed and set the timer so when they got up it had brewed and was piping hot. Tonight it was up to her.

She scooped heaping spoons of beans into the grinder and set it whirring, her emotions spinning as fast as the blade. She didn't care if Cash was in the family room and could hear her. She gave in and had the good, hard cry she'd been fighting since Opa's disappearance. Her body convulsed with the pain. She released the grinder to wrap her arms around her stomach.

"Don't cry, honey." Cash came up behind her and gently turned her to face him. "It'll be okay."

At his kindness, her crying increased. He drew her into his arms and held her. She snuggled against him and felt a semblance of peace. She still wished he'd tell her about the parts of his past that he was withholding, but she was starting to believe that he really was exactly what he portrayed himself to be. A good, honest and decent man who'd be there for her whenever she needed him. Just as he'd been there for others when he was in the military. And now, as a deputy, putting others before himself, risking his life all the time.

The doorbell rang.

She pulled back in fear.

"Relax," he said with a sweet smile. "Criminals don't ring doorbells."

Despite her tension, she laughed through choked sobs.

"You stay here. I'll get the door." He kissed her forehead and stepped out of the room.

She grabbed tissues from a box on the counter. As she made herself presentable, she heard male voices in a heated conversation. She waited for Cash to call out for her, but when he didn't, she went down the hall to see who was at the door. He stood by the sofa with one of the detectives who'd investigated Toby's murder.

Just the sight of Detective Eason sent blood draining from her head.

Eason pinned Cash with a glare. "If you didn't want this to happen, then you shouldn't have told me Mrs. Alger was back in town."

Krista felt as if she'd been slapped across the face. She hurried back to the kitchen. Cash, the man who'd stood by her side, who'd just kissed her forehead and made it seem as if he cared, had failed to tell her he'd talked to Eason. And even worse, he ratted her out. How could she have considered trusting him? How had she been so wrong again?

He stepped into the kitchen and didn't seem the least bit apologetic for bringing Eason back into her life. "A detective working Toby's investigation is here. He has some questions for you."

She was too exhausted to ask why he'd betrayed her this way. She woodenly walked to the family room and perched on the edge of a chair. "What do you want to know?"

"Glad to see you wised up and came back to town." Eason stood towering over her. "Where have you been the last few years?"

She filled him in on her life in Kennesaw, sticking to the facts but telling him everything lest he accuse her of not being truthful. Eason took notes on his little pad, scribbling away as if he was afraid to miss a single word.

When she finished her story, he looked up and smirked. "Pretty smart using the false ID that Daddy got for you. What else did you use Daddy's connections for? Maybe to hide the money in some offshore account?"

Krista crossed her arms. "I've told you, like, a thousand times, I did not touch that money."

"Then when we request your banking information for Georgia we won't find you lived the high life."

"Right." Krista scoffed. "The high life all child-care givers live on minimum wage."

"So where's the money?" he snapped at her.

Cash stepped closer. "No need to be so harsh, Detective."

She ignored Cash's attempt to help. "Believe me. If I knew where it was, I'd tell you."

"We'll see what your recent finances turn up and talk again. You can count on that." Eason nodded at Cash, then stormed out of the house.

Cash locked the door and turned to Krista. "I'm sorry he was so rude. He shouldn't treat you like that. He's frustrated with it taking so long to close this case."

"You would stick up for him, wouldn't you?"

"What?"

"You told him about me." She got to her feet. "I'm such a fool. I honestly thought you cared about me, but you called Eason. How could you?"

He tried to respond, but she held up a hand, stopping him. "Don't bother," she said, already on her way to the hallway. "There's nothing you could say that would help."

"Krista, wait," he called after her. "It wasn't like that at all. Let me explain."

She fired a look over her shoulder. "How do you explain betrayal, Cash? How?"

She marched into her room and slammed her door. She paced like a penned dog. She couldn't wait for tomorrow when she would deliver the flash drive, they'd catch the bomber and Opa would be freed. Then she could get Cash out of her life before she actually fell hard for another man who broke her trust.

Cash, the team and Krista sat at the conference room table the next morning. Techs had connected the phone left at Erwin's house to a recording device with speakers and placed it in the middle of the table. The room was tense and, at times, Cash felt as if all the air had been sucked out of the space.

He wasn't surprised. If the wait for the bomber's call wasn't enough to make him uneasy, the tension between him and Krista would do so. He looked at her. Her lips were pinched, her eyes narrowed. He'd heard her walking the floor last night and knew she hadn't gotten much sleep. Neither had he. He'd tried to talk to her over breakfast, but she wouldn't listen. Worst part was he understood why she felt this way. Her father had lied to her. Her husband had lied, too, and left her in a terrible position. So she'd immediately jumped to the wrong conclusion about him. He'd likely do the same thing in her situation.

The phone rang, and she jerked up in her seat.

"Showtime." A nervous energy buzzed around Skyler as she looked at Krista. "You know what to say. Do your best to keep him talking." Skyler hovered her finger over the talk button. "Ready?"

Krista nodded and when Skyler pressed the button, Krista leaned over the phone. "I have what you asked for."

"Good." A voice scrambler disguised the male voice coming over the speaker. "We'll meet at Pioneer Square in one hour. Bring this phone. There's a bench with one slat painted yellow on the end. Leave the item in the envelope underneath. Then wait by Umbrella Man for further directions. Come alone and we'll make the trade. Bring others…"

Cash looked at Jake, waiting for him to shoot down the idea of a lunchtime meeting at Pioneer Square, home to the famous bronze statue of a man offering his umbrella to visitors. The large bowl-shaped area sank into the ground downtown, affectionately called Portland's living room, would be teeming with people. It would be hard to control an exchange and the sunken amphitheater could trap Krista.

Jake remained quiet.

"I need proof that you have my grandfather," Krista said as Skyler had instructed her. "I need to hear his voice."

"Okay, old man—" the bomber's voice grew fainter "—say hello to your granddaughter."

"Do not do this," Opa's voice came over the speaker.

Cash saw Krista nearly collapse in her chair. "Are you okay, Opa? Did he hurt you?"

"I am fine, but do not give this man what he wants."

"Sit down, old man," the bomber said. "I presume you'll choose to ignore him. One hour. After I confirm you've delivered the right information, you'll see him alive. Bring that cop who's been hanging out with you and it's over."

The line went dead.

Skyler looked up from the recording equipment. "Not long enough for a trace, but if he used a cell, I'll try to get the GPS. Maybe we can wrap this up before Krista has to meet him."

"You go do that," Jake said. "We'll strategize the exchange."

"I don't like this." Cash shoved a hand into his hair and paced. "Putting Krista in a space we can't control is risky. The bomber could easily blend in with the lunchtime crowd and kill her to keep her from testifying against him."

"He's had plenty of chances to kill her," Archer pointed out. "I doubt that's his endgame."

"We'll also fit her with a vest," Jake added.

Not good enough. "I know I can't go in her place, but let's send a female deputy instead."

"No." Krista crossed her arms. "I won't let a deputy risk her life instead of me. And if the kidnapper realizes she's taken my place, Opa's life would be in danger, too. This is my responsibility."

Cash didn't want her to go, but he respected

her willingness to give up her life for her family. He wanted someone with such amazing love in his life again. Sure, he had the FRS guys, but he wanted someone to come home to at the end of every day. Someone waiting for him and him alone.

"Are you sure you're good to do this?" he asked, giving her an out.

She nodded. "He has Opa. I'd do anything to get him back, even if it means I'm killed in the process."

"If you die, honey..." Cash paused to make eye contact so she understood his commitment to keeping her safe. "It means they've gone through me first and I'm not alive to protect you."

Cash had hoped that Skyler would be able to trace the bomber's phone, but it was a disposable and didn't produce another lead. They'd had no good explanation for the algorithm, either. So, despite Cash's misgivings, he helped the FRS set up at Pioneer Square.

The air was crisp and cold, and a fine mist fell, darkening the red bricks. First, they'd cleared the area of pedestrians and cordoned it off using county trucks to make it look as if his teammates were utility workers repairing a water main. The bomber might get suspicious, but better that than risk having him show up wearing a suicide vest and take out innocent people.

The bomber claimed on the phone that he'd recognize Cash, so he couldn't show his face. He'd found a hidden location near the MAX train tracks. The rest of the team had taken strategic positions surrounding the square.

As Cash watched through his binoculars, Krista worked her way down the stairs leading into the amphitheater and approached the drop spot. Step by step she walked toward the yellow slat shining like a beacon.

Cash held his breath, waiting for disaster to strike. His heart thundered in his ears. Never had fear like this threatened to destroy him.

He couldn't lose Krista. He just couldn't.

Oh, man. He'd fallen for her hook, line and sinker and now he could lose her.

She sat down and reached under the bench. He saw her slide the card into an envelope attached to the bottom. She got up and calmly strolled to the Umbrella Man. Cash was so proud of her strength, but he didn't have time to dwell on it. He had to make sure they caught the bomber and brought Otto home safely.

"Package delivered," he said into his mic and kept watch on the bench.

Time passed slowly, each second sounding in his head.

Finally, a male fitting the bomber's description approached the bench and sat down. Cash ran his gaze over the guy's chest, looking for the bulky vest pictured on the flash drive. Found nothing. Good. No suicide vest.

"Suspect in place," Cash told the team. "He's not wearing a vest. Repeat, not wearing a vest. Be ready."

The man snatched the envelope. Opened it. Smiled and got up. He stepped to a bike rack, grabbed a ten-speed and started pedaling toward the opposite side of the square from Krista.

"He's making a run for it," Cash shouted. "Go, go, go."

His teammates kicked into action, moving closer, tightening their circle until the bomber was in the middle.

"Now," Cash said.

They drew their weapons.

"Police," Jake shouted. "On the ground, now!"

"Me?" the man asked, appearing genuinely surprised.

Brady seized the moment, grabbed the guy's arm, took him down and cuffed him.

"I'll get Krista so she can ID him," Cash announced over his mic, then barreled over to Krista.

"You should have waited before apprehending him," she cried out. "What about Opa?"

"We couldn't wait. The suspect was taking off." Cash took her hand. Her body trembled as they hurried across the bricks.

The closer they came to the suspect, the more her hand shook.

"Turn him around, Brady," Cash directed.

The guy pivoted.

Krista clutched her chest. "It's not him. Oh, no. No, no, no. We have the wrong guy and the bomber's going to kill Opa."

A slash of anguish cut into Cash. "Who sent you?" he shouted at the suspect.

He shrugged. "Don't know his name and didn't see the guy."

"You expect me to believe you don't know him?"

"I was hired from Craigslist to pick up the package. We handled everything via email. Honest. You can look at my phone if you don't believe me."

"Why would we believe you?" Cash started for the creep and planned to make him talk.

Skyler stepped forward and cast a warning look at Cash, telling him to back off. "I'll haul him down to County to get to the bottom of this. We'll track these supposed phone and email contacts. Hopefully it will lead to our bomber."

"Dude," the guy said, "is this really about a bomber?"

Skyler nodded.

"How cool is that?"

"Not cool at all." She grabbed the man's handcuffs. "Let's go."

Skyler and Brady departed with the suspect, who dragged his feet. The rest of the team stood by, but none of them offered an idea of how to find Otto—the sweet, kind man who didn't deserve to be held hostage. Cash felt powerless to help Krista and he knew he was letting her down. As he'd let down his Delta team. The helpless feeling made his gut hurt.

She suddenly clutched his arm. "We could use the phone the bomber left to call him. I could redial the last number called."

"I doubt he'll answer."

"I have to try." Krista dialed and lifted the phone to her ear.

The team members watched, all of them eagerly awaiting the result.

Krista listened intently, then frowned. "The number's no longer in service." She turned in a circle, her eyes wide with worry. "We have to do something before he kills Opa."

"I'm sorry, Krista," Jake said. "But all we can do right now is head back to County and hope Skyler finds something in those emails."

"We can pray," Cash offered, surprising himself. "Pray for Otto's safety and that the bomber calls again."

TWENTY-ONE

Cash settled into his makeshift bed on Krista's couch and checked his service weapon to make sure it was loaded and ready, then rested it on his chest and propped an arm behind his head. Time had passed slowly—painfully—today without a call from the bomber or any leads from Skyler's investigation. Everyone on the team had come to care for Otto and their concern for his well-being mounted.

Then there was Krista. She was near hysterics and wouldn't let Cash offer any comfort. She was still mad at him for talking to the detective. He'd wanted to explain the misunderstanding, but he didn't want to bring it up and add additional turmoil to her life.

He sighed out his frustration and snapped off the light. He heard the wind jostling the trees. The usual rain hitting the windows. Krista moving around in her room, not settling down until 2:00 a.m. Hopefully, she'd get some rest, but Cash doubted it.

His phone rang from the table, and he shot

to his feet. Jake's name appeared on the screen. Worry ramping up, Cash answered.

"We received a callout for a bomb threat at a construction company." Jake gave the address. "We need you to meet us there."

"I can't leave Krista alone," Cash said, though as the only bomb tech on the team, he had to go or someone else could die.

"Brady's already en route to relieve you. Should be on your doorstep any minute."

"Then I'm on my way." Cash hung up and went down the hall to Krista's room. He knocked on the door.

She opened it, wearing a big fluffy robe.

He told her about the bomb. "I have to go."

Fear shone plainly on her face, touching Cash's heart.

"Don't worry," he said. "Brady will stay with you."

"I'm not worried about me. It's you... You could... A bomb."

"You're worried about me?"

She nodded and looked down at her feet.

He crooked a finger under her chin and tipped her head up. "You know I meant no harm in calling Eason, right? I wanted to help you."

She didn't say anything, but kept her gaze riveted to him.

"I get that after Toby lied to you, and you don't trust easily. I hope you'll give me a chance to prove you can trust me." He touched her cheek. Felt the softness. Saw the look of indecision in her eyes. A callout could go badly. Each event was a risk. If something bad happened, this wasn't how he wanted to remember her.

"I care about you, Krista," he whispered and before she could stop him, he swooped in to kiss her.

As he put every emotion he'd been battling into the kiss, he heard pounding on the front door. He lifted his head. Krista opened her eyes. They were soft, dreamy and filled with longing.

Oh, yeah, this was better. So much better. This was how he wanted to remember her if things went south.

"I'll let Brady in." He kissed her again, quickly but decisively, before answering the door. A sleepy Brady stood yawning and scratching his head.

"You stay alert." Cash poked his friend in the chest. "No snoozing on the job."

"I got this. A cup of coffee and I'm good to go."

"You'll have to answer to me if anything goes wrong here." Cash let his warning look linger until he was certain Brady took his responsibility seriously. "Call me if anything, and I mean anything, happens."

"Like I said, I got it. So keep your mind on the bomb not on us."

Cash jogged down the steps and soon had his car on the road. He wasn't surprised to see the construction office was nothing more than a double-wide trailer sitting on blocks. The FRS truck was parked at the end of the driveway, well away from the trailer for safety. Wally the robot sat outside, and Jake stood near the FRS truck talking with Skyler.

Cash crossed over to them. "What do we have?"

"The owner's inside strapped to a chair and wearing a suicide vest with a timer ticking down." Jake ground his teeth.

"A vest?" Cash let the thought ruminate. "Like the vest on the bomber's flash drive?"

"Let's focus on rendering this bomb safe before talking about any connection to Krista," Jake said.

"You don't need any distractions," Skyler added.

Jake looked at his watch. "According to the 911 call made by the worker who found the owner, we have less than thirty minutes on the timer. The owner—Upjohn—said there weren't any other devices inside."

"I still need to check it out. Let me get Wally going." Cash climbed into the truck and soon had the robot on the move. After a thorough search of the building's exterior, Cash sent Wally inside and panned the room with his camera, finally settling on Upjohn. He sat in a metal chair, his hands tied behind, his feet strapped to the legs of the chair. Cash looked for a remote detonator in Upjohn's hands, near his feet, his knees, anywhere he could simply press a device. Cash had to make sure this wasn't a suicide mission meant to take out a bomb tech. Namely him.

After a thorough search, Cash was confident it was safe to enter the building. He climbed into his suit with Skyler's help.

When she'd fixed the last Velcro strap, she patted him on the shoulder. "Take care in there."

He nodded and she settled the helmet on his head. He crossed the lot to the trailer. Giving Upjohn a thumbs-up as he approached, Cash once again confirmed the lack of remotes, then checked to be certain there wasn't a pressure device keeping Upjohn in the chair. Believing it safe to proceed, he turned his attention to the vest. The device had similarities in materials and design to the stadium bomb. It also matched the schematics they'd looked at last night minus the handheld trigger, but Cash couldn't focus on that with only ten minutes left on the timer.

He went to work, finishing his job with three minutes to spare. He unstrapped the device and gently set it on the floor. He helped Upjohn to his feet and pointed at the exit. The man literally ran for the door. Cash had to move slower. Darcie already had Upjohn sitting on the truck bumper with a blood pressure cuff attached to his arm by the time Cash reached them.

Skyler helped Cash shed his suit. He gestured for Jake and Skyler to join him out of Upjohn's hearing range. "Before you call MEDU to dispose of the explosives, you should know I believe the device was made by the stadium bomber."

"Believe?" Skyler asked.

"Can never be positive from a visual inspection, but the similarities can't be overlooked. With Otto missing, we can't afford to wait for an analysis to confirm it."

Jake furrowed his brow. "We need to question Upjohn."

Cash's feeling exactly, and he wasted no time heading back to the man.

"Is he good to answer a few questions?" Cash asked Darcie.

She looked at Upjohn. "Mr. Upjohn—"

"Would you people quit calling me that?" he interrupted. "Name's Steve."

Darcie smiled at him. "Steve is doing remarkably well."

"Not like I haven't been around explosives before."

Cash admired the man's attitude. "What can you tell us about the person who strapped you into the vest?"

"White guy. Skinny. Maybe six feet. Wore a ski mask. His eyes were this weird blue color. Almost gray."

Skyler brought up the bomber's sketch on her phone and handed it to Steve. "This the guy?"

"Could be, but with the mask, I can't be sure."

"What *are* you sure of?" Cash asked.

"I'm sure he hated me. Glared at me the whole time. That's why I remember his eyes so well. Said I would pay for my carelessness on the stadium renovation."

"Stadium," Skyler said. "What stadium?"

"It's Providence Park now but it was Jeld-Wen Field when we worked on the renovation. As far as carelessness goes…" He shook his head. "Only thing I can think this guy is talking about is one of our workers hurt his back in an explosion and ended up disabled. OSHA cleared us. It was just a freak accident."

Skyler pulled out her notebook. "Do you remember the guy's name?"

"Hugo Ketchum."

Skyler's eyes lit up. "You're sure about the name?"

"Yeah. He worked for me for ten years. Was a hard worker, and I was sorry to see him go, but the back injury disabled him permanently." Steve shook his head. "I didn't even blame him when he sued the company and the stadium. Probably would've done the same thing if I was in his shoes. But as I said, we were cleared of any negligence."

"Bet that made Hugo mad," Cash said.

"Mad's not the word for it. But that was years ago, and I never heard from him again. If this is related to Hugo, I don't know why he waited so long." Steve held up a hand. "Don't get me wrong. I don't think Hugo was the guy who put the vest on me. I could tell by his hands that he was much younger."

"There's a Ketchum on the stadium employee list," Skyler said. "I remember the name because it made me think of ketchup. Could Hugo work there?"

Steve shook his head. "His son Leo could, though. He'd be in his late twenties by now."

"Any idea where Leo and Hugo live?"

"Sorry. No."

"Anything else that might help us locate this man?" Skyler asked.

Steve tapped his chin. "Not really. But I'll keep thinking about it."

Skyler gave him her card and gestured for Cash and Jake to join her away from the vehicle. "My files are back at the firehouse. I don't want to waste any time before looking for Leo Ketchum. Cash can drive me over there while the scene gets wrapped up."

Jake nodded. "We'll meet you back at the house."

Skyler started off, but Cash lingered. He felt as if he was missing something, but he didn't know what. Maybe he just didn't want to leave the man who had provided their best lead in case Steve remembered something else.

Skyler turned back. "What are you waiting for, Cash? We finally have a strong lead, and we might be able to arrest our bomber before daybreak."

* * *

"The warrant's here." Skyler waved the form in the air. "Let's roll and bring this guy in."

Cash felt his excitement mount as the rest of the FRS team jumped to their feet and headed for the firehouse door. They'd discovered Leo Ketchum's name on the stadium employee list and emailed his photo to Krista, who'd positively identified him as their bomber. Skyler located Ketchum's address and obtained an arrest warrant plus a warrant to search his room.

Finally, they were likely going to bring Otto home, and Cash wanted to tell Krista to ease her mind. Maybe to ease his own mind that she was there waiting for him.

He'd had plenty of time to think about her while waiting for the warrant. About her care for her preschoolers. For Otto. The way a simple look from her made his heart fire. She was an amazing woman and he had to follow these feelings for her. He didn't know if Krista would have him—she had a lot to get over first. So did he, but maybe when this was all over, he could put Opa's advice into practice and trust God to help him let go of his past, then they could see where this thing between them led.

He stepped outside and held up his phone. "I need a minute to make a quick call."

Skyler eyed him. "One minute, then I'm leaving without you."

He quickly dialed Krista and brought her up-to-date.

"You found the bomber. You really found him." She sounded breathless with excitement.

"Hopefully he hasn't moved. We're headed out to make the arrest now. I wanted to check in with you before going. I could come back there instead if you want me to."

"No, go after this guy and rescue Opa. That's the most important thing."

Skyler peered at him from the back of the truck and tapped her watch. Cash started for the truck. "Let me talk to Brady."

"I'll get him."

"Yo," Brady said a moment later.

"Everything okay there?"

"Relax, man." Brady's voice was calm and confident. "We're fine."

Cash told Brady about the warrant and made him reaffirm his promise to call if anything came up. Feeling optimistic, Cash stowed his phone and climbed into the truck. Jake was behind the wheel as usual, the truck already running. Archer rode shotgun. The others sat in the middle and Cash joined them.

"Ketchum rents a room at a boardinghouse owned by a Glenda Yapp," Skyler was saying.

"Not the best part of town," Jake commented and didn't wait for Cash to sit before merging into traffic.

Skyler nodded. "Not surprising if they were living off Hugo's disability check and Leo's minimum-wage job at the stadium."

Cash added, "Sounds like a good reason for revenge."

"I don't know." Archer turned to look at them. "If that's Ketchum's reasoning, I understand going after Upjohn, but bombing a stadium, where innocent people would die? That doesn't fit."

"It does if he was targeting a spectator," Cash said.

"I suppose," Archer replied. "But I think it would need to be more than that."

The team fell silent as the tires spun over the wet pavement and the long wipers swiped across the window. Cash assumed everyone was thinking about this guy's obsession with explosives and whether he'd used them on Otto.

"Ten minutes out," Jake announced.

They silently donned their Kevlar vests and checked their weapons. When the truck pulled to the curb in a run-down neighborhood, they were ready for action.

Jake cut off the engine and assessed the building. "Archer and Skyler cover the back. Cash and I'll take the front."

They stepped down from the truck and moved swiftly and decisively. Jake pounded on the front door.

A stout woman with messy gray hair needing a good washing answered.

Jake displayed his ID. "We're looking for a Leo and Hugo Ketchum."

"Not here." She stifled a yawn as if she had deputies arriving on her doorstep all the time.

"Do you know where we can find them?" Cash asked.

"No idea about Leo, but Hugo's dead and buried."

"Dead? When?" Cash asked.

"Last week. Guy was in terrible pain all the time. He went to the hospital to have a morphine pump implanted in his back to relieve it, but he got an infection and never recovered."

Hugo's death was the perfect reason for Leo to start taking revenge after such a long time. Jake's knowing expression said he thought so, too.

"When's the last time you saw Leo?" Jake asked.

"Not since Sunday. The guy's rent is due, and I figure he's hiding out 'cause he doesn't have it." She scowled. "I wasn't going to toss him out right after Hugo's passing, but the kid don't need to know that."

Cash's hope plummeted. If she hadn't seen Ketchum for three days, that meant Otto wasn't here.

"We have a warrant to search their room." Cash half expected her to close the door in their face.

She stepped back. "First door at the top of the stairs."

"My associates would also like to have a look around the house."

She frowned. "Now, why would I let you do that?"

Jake stepped forward. "If you don't, I'll come back with a warrant for that, too. You should know that will make my deputies cranky. You don't want to deal with cranky deputies, do you?"

"Fine," she said. "But leave my things be."

Jake called Skyler and Archer to the front. They started through the first level while Jake and Cash climbed the stairs to Ketchum's room. It held an old iron bed with a well-worn quilt, scarred dresser and matching nightstand. A single lightbulb hung from above, casting shadows in the room.

"Let's tear this place apart," Jake said eagerly.

"Not like there's much to tear apart."

Cash went through the nightstand while Jake searched the dresser. Nothing. Cash dropped to the dingy carpet to look under the bed. He pulled out a few boxes and dug through them. Nothing again.

Angry at coming up empty, he shoved the last box and hit the bed frame. A clanking noise sounded from one of the posts.

"You hear that?" Cash asked.

Jake was already shaking the bed. "The corner

post is hollow. There's something in it. I'll lift up the bed, you unscrew the foot."

Cash twisted the rusty foot from the post and a key dropped out. He looked at the tag. "It's for a storage place. Unit 23. Just down the street."

Excitement sparked in Jake's eyes. "You think that's where Leo's hiding Otto?"

"Wouldn't Leo have the key with him if he was?"

"Maybe this key belonged to the father."

"Worth checking out."

They quickly looked through the other rooms on the second floor, then met Skyler and Archer outside. Cash didn't have to ask if they'd found Otto. Their sullen expressions said it all. They climbed into the truck and within minutes pulled up to the storage facility. They left the truck near the entrance and crept toward the long building.

"Over there," Cash whispered and pointed at a unit where light shone from under a cracked-open door.

Jake gestured for them to fall back, and they circled together.

"Two scenarios I can see," he said. "Otto's inside alone or Ketchum's with him."

Cash appreciated that Jake didn't even entertain the idea that Otto wasn't here. "We can't simply breach the place and risk Otto's life."

"We could get a snake camera inside without him seeing it," Skyler suggested.

"I'll get it." Cash ran back to the truck before anyone else could volunteer. If he took control of the camera and spotted Otto inside, Cash planned to be the first one through the door to rescue the sweet old guy and maybe lay Ketchum out in the process.

Krista hung out in the family room, staring out the window. Waiting for Opa to arrive home had given her time to calm down. To compose herself. To take the time to pray and reflect on her life. She now possessed an insight she'd never had before.

Worrying was pointless. So was trying to control things she had no power over. She'd worked hard to plan for what could happen to her once she returned to Portland. Had even prepared her escape if needed. But God saw fit to let others thwart her plans.

That meant only one thing to her. She'd come to the end of what she could do for herself and had to listen to Opa and let go. Let go of the worry. Let go of the strife, or she'd spend a lifetime needlessly worrying.

"Watching won't bring them back faster," Brady said from the sofa. "Besides, it's not a good idea to stand in front of the window."

She spun. "They have the bomber in custody. How's he going to hurt me from there?"

"You *think* they have him in custody. We don't have confirmation yet. And if that's not enough to get you to move, think about Cash. Would he let you stand there under these conditions?"

She thought about his deep need to protect her. "No, but—"

"He'll see you when he pulls in the driveway. I'd rather you move away from the window than have to explain why I let you stay there." Brady grinned.

She saw headlights flash into the driveway, and she bolted to the door.

"Wait," Brady warned. "It might not be Cash."

Brady joined her, and they both watched out the side window.

"That's not Cash's car. Stay here. I'll check this out." Brady stepped outside and closed the door.

Krista heard him talking with another man before he poked his head in the house. "Guy's name is Ian Summers. Says he's an old college friend of Toby's and claims to have important information about Toby's murder."

"Then let him in," Krista said eagerly and went to greet Toby's friend.

Krista immediately recognized the short, powerfully built man who entered carrying a briefcase.

"I don't know if you remember me," Ian said.

"Yes, of course." She shook hands with him. "You came to our wedding. Please come in."

Krista motioned for Ian to sit on the sofa. As he settled in, she sat next to him and introduced

Ian to Brady, who leaned against the wall watching carefully.

Krista turned her attention to Ian. "You have information about Toby's death?"

"I do." He rested the briefcase on his lap, then snapped it open and rummaged around.

Krista chewed on her lip and hoped the evidence he was retrieving could solve Toby's murder and finally clear her name. Couple that with the bomber being arrested and Opa coming home and her life was finally looking up.

Ian glanced over the briefcase at her. Smiled. She returned the smile and then looked back at the case. Waiting. Eager.

His hand shot out. A small gun was clasped in stubby fingers. He jabbed it into Krista's side before she could do anything but gasp.

His smile widened into a sick, twisted grimace. "I know all about how Toby died. I'm the one who killed him."

TWENTY-TWO

Jake took a stance in front of the storage door while Cash stood behind him wearing his EOD suit. They had to go in quick and precise to keep Ketchum from taking the place down. Their camera had revealed him sitting alone at a table filled with explosives. They couldn't risk harming him, or they may never learn where he'd stashed Otto, but they also couldn't risk stepping inside without protection. Jake would slide the door up, then move out of harm's way, and Cash would go in gun drawn.

It was risky, but a risk Cash and Jake would willingly take for Otto. Hopefully, Ketchum wouldn't be able to react faster than the team.

Jake nodded at Cash, then slid the door open.

Ketchum looked up from behind the long metal table. Cash charged and had his gun to Ketchum's head within moments. He hauled Ketchum to his feet and dragged him away from the explosives. Outside, Cash shoved him to the ground and pressed his face into the concrete as the team came charging in.

Jake cuffed Ketchum, and as soon as he'd read him his rights, he asked, "Where's Otto?"

"Who?" Ketchum asked.

Jake got in Ketchum's face. "Otto Schiffer. The man you kidnapped."

"I didn't kidnap anyone."

Cash's anger flared, and he reached up to jerk off his helmet so he could have a go at the creep.

Jake grabbed his arm. "Before we do anything else, go clear the place in case we have a ticking timer inside."

Cash would rather stay and pummel Ketchum, but he headed into the unit. Didn't take long for him to see that Ketchum was building another device but hadn't activated it. Cash sifted through papers and found blueprints next to supplies that were of the same specifications as the other bombs, but no impending explosion. Back outside, he gave a thumbs-up. Skyler removed his helmet, and Cash pulled the quick-release toggle to shed his suit so he could get his hands on Ketchum.

"Found blueprints for the stadium and construction office. Plus diagrams for a suicide vest." Cash stepped closer to Ketchum. "You're making another bomb. Who's this one for?"

"Wouldn't you like to know?" Ketchum sneered.

"Look, creep." Jake suddenly bent over Ketchum. "We have enough to put you away for a very long time. We know you set the stadium bomb and put the vest on Upjohn to get revenge for your father's death. But if Otto dies, that's a whole other thing. I'll make sure you never see the light of day. You get me?" He tugged on Ketchum's shirt. "So knock off the wise-guy stuff and answer our questions."

"Seriously, I don't know who this Otto guy is," Ketchum replied, sounding truthful.

Cash charged at him, but Jake stepped in the way. "Then tell me what you do know about. Like these supplies, Upjohn and the stadium."

"They all got away with killing my dad," he said, emotion raw in his voice. "Sure, the stupid doctor was ultimately to blame, but the others killed him when they decided to cut corners." He shook his head, his eyes burning with hatred.

Archer moved closer. "And you want them to pay."

Ketchum nodded.

"But something went wrong at the stadium," Archer continued and Ketchum stared as if in a trance.

"It was me," he said. "I screwed up. I was after the stadium manager who signed the contract with Upjohn Construction. Only him, but he's such a big baby he couldn't sit out in the rain." Ketchum swung his head sorrowfully. "He let my dad work in every kind of weather condition, but no, he couldn't handle a little rain. So I moved locations. But I should've waited for a better chance. Then

I wouldn't have run into the freaky woman who reported me."

Archer moved closer. "The woman you've been stalking all week."

Ketchum's eyes opened wide. "What? No. I'll admit to breaking into her house to retrieve my flash drive, but she woke up and screamed."

"And that's when you tried to abduct her?"

"Abduct her? No, you're nuts. *She* came after *me*."

"Then why drag her toward the door?"

"I was just trying to get out of the house. But, man, she was a pit bull. Couldn't get away from her so I took her with me. Once I got the door open, I planned to shove her down and run." He shook his head. "No way I'd try to take that woman. No way."

Cash had to smile at how tenacious Krista had been.

"So then you came back the next day," Archer said, resuming his role.

"Yeah, for the coat she'd worn to the stadium, but it wasn't in the house."

"And that's when you started following her and planted a detonator in the couch to make her look guilty," Skyler stated.

"Really? Where are you people getting these crazy stories? I didn't plant anything."

Cash felt like taking the guy's head off for his

continued attitude, but held his temper. "How'd you find her in the first place?"

"You're a cop and you have to ask?" He smirked. "I tailed you when you drove her home."

Cash clenched his jaw and warred with the guilt of letting this guy get to her. "You expect us to believe you just gave up looking for the flash drive?"

"Dude, after you stuck to her like glue I wasn't gonna risk getting caught for a stupid drive."

Cash eyed the man. "If it was so stupid, why give it to her in the first place, then come looking for it?"

"The crazy lady mentioned my backpack, I figured she'd get nosy and report me, and I didn't want the cops stopping me on the way out. My bomb schematics would get me hauled downtown. I can always figure out a new algorithm to beat the lottery, but I can't plant a bomb from jail."

"The lottery? This is about winning the lottery?" Skyler said in disgust and crossed her arms.

"You claim this algorithm is important," Cash moved on. "So why carry it with you?"

"I shouldn't have, but what else was I supposed to do with it? I couldn't leave it here. Something could explode and destroy it. And Yapp goes through our rooms. She doesn't think I know about it, but all her boarders know. She searches top to bottom. Anyway, I have to work on my algorithm on library computers and the drive makes it easy to store my information."

"Ever hear of cloud storage?" Skyler said sarcastically.

"Sure, hasn't everyone? But I can't leave a trail behind at the library. Not if I planned to pull this off and beat the lottery, too. Too risky."

"So you wanted the drive back because the algorithm would let you win the lottery?" Jake clarified.

Ketchum nodded. "I'm nearly there. A few more days work and I would have it."

Skyler gestured for the team to join her away from Ketchum.

"You move one inch, and I'll let Deputy Dixon have at you," Jake warned Ketchum.

Skyler leaned closer and kept her voice down. "Do you guys think Ketchum is as innocent as he's making himself sound?"

"I'm not sure what vibe I'm getting from him." Archer narrowed his eyes. "He admitted to all the bombings. Why not confess to the incidents at Krista's house and kidnapping Otto if he did them? Especially after Jake put him in his place."

"Because kidnapping adds a whole new level to his crimes." Skyler settled her hands on her hips. "We need to keep after him just in case he's leading us astray."

"Then let's get him down to County for further questioning," Archer said.

Cash nodded his agreement. "I'll go with you."

Jake shook his head. "Not a good idea. You can hardly keep your hands off the guy."

"Tough." Cash crossed his arms. "I won't go back to Krista until I know Otto's location, so don't even bother trying to stop me."

Krista stared at Ian in stunned disbelief. With his eye on her, he'd forced Brady to his stomach on the floor and searched him, removing two guns. Then he'd held Krista at gunpoint and made her haul two dining chairs into the middle of the room. He'd tied Brady to one of them. Next, he'd bound Krista's wrists with thick cable ties and shoved her onto the chair beside Brady.

"Why are you doing this, Ian?" Krista asked.

He blinked in surprise. "Really, you have to ask? I want my money and you're finally going to tell me where it is."

"Money, what money?"

He turned and glared at her, his eyes hot with anger. "Like you don't know. The half million you moved from your bank account."

"You were involved in the scam?"

"Involved." He sneered, his face contorted in ugliness. "It was all my idea. I'm the one who convinced Toby to join me. You wouldn't have had your fancy car or pretty clothes without me. He was such a loser. Could never think outside the box. Let his goody-goody Christian morals control him. Which is why I didn't tell him what I was really doing." His lips tipped in a mocking smile. "It was so amazing to see him excited about the company, only to learn he'd been living off seniors' retirement funds."

"Then he didn't lie to me." Guilt flooded Krista's heart for not believing in him.

"Oh, he lied to you, all right. First, about being involved." Ian faked a gag. "He wanted to surprise you with a European vacation so he kept it all a secret. Then, when he found out what I was up to, he was too embarrassed to tell you. Wanted to wait until he turned me in to the cops and made things right."

How could she have doubted Toby's innocence? She'd been so wrong about him.

"If he was too innocent for you," Brady said, "why involve him in the first place?"

"Schemes like these eventually go bust." Ian turned his attention to Brady. "You more than anyone should know that, copper. One disgruntled investor gets the SEC involved. Things snowball. People go to jail. But not me. I had it all planned with Toby as my fall guy. I structured everything in his name and made sure he deposited all the money. But he discovered what I was up to and threatened to go to the police. I had to stop him. That meant Toby had to die. At least one thing went right—the detectives never figured out Toby had a partner."

"So you killed him, but how?" Brady asked.

Ian smiled again, his pride evident. Krista could see Brady was trying to elicit a full confession from Ian, but he was too full of himself to realize what Brady was doing. Or he didn't care because he didn't plan to let either one of them live.

The thought sent terror to Krista's heart.

"Toby was so stressed out he was taking Valium—another secret he kept from you. When we met for a drink late that night, I added a bit of GHB. Deadly combo." He turned his focus to Krista. "When he started having trouble breathing I brought him home and dumped him into bed to set you up for the murder." His grin disappeared. "Enough with the explaining. I know Toby moved the money to your joint account before threatening to report me to the police."

"Maybe you should've thought of that before you killed him," Brady said.

Ian turned on Brady and backhanded him. "You think I'm such a fool that I'd kill him with the money missing? I had no idea he'd moved it until after I killed him."

Brady smirked. "Maybe you should've checked."

Another crack to Brady's face, but he didn't even flinch, just smiled up at Ian.

Brady might have doubted her innocence, but

she respected the strength and determination he was exhibiting on her behalf.

"Leave Brady alone," Krista called out. "He had nothing to do with this."

"You're right." Ian stepped menacingly toward Krista. "It's all on you. I didn't count on you taking off after I trashed your house while looking for the account information."

"That was you, too? Not my neighbors?" Krista swallowed hard. "But why the hateful messages?"

Ian laughed. "I planned it that way so you wouldn't suspect anyone had searched your house. Just like planting the detonator at your house this week. I had to make the cops think you were involved in the bombing to keep them from suspecting that I was looking for something. If I'd only known you had a grandfather before now, I would've kidnapped him and had my money years ago. Now that I have him, maybe you'll sing a different tune to get him back."

"Opa? *You* took Opa?" Krista's heart dropped to her stomach.

"Yes, and if you'd given me the location of the money at Pioneer Square like I'd asked, your grandfather would be here and I wouldn't."

They had been wrong about so many things, and now Opa might pay for it. "Where's my grandfather?"

"Don't worry. He's fine. I made sure he didn't

see me. I'll release him after you hand over the account information. If you love him, you'll comply."

Brady looked at her. "On the other hand, *we've* seen Ian, so you know what he plans to do with us."

Ian grinned, a sick, mean slash of his lips. "But not until I have my money, of course."

"I can't give you what I don't have," Krista said, her own voice so frantic it scared her.

"Still sticking to that story?" Ian let out a frustrated sigh. "Okay, have it your way. You won't be able to stay quiet for long. Not with what I have planned." Ian jerked her up by the cable ties, his face twisted in anger. "You'd be surprised at what a little time in an icy river can do to lower your resolve."

The creep Ketchum refused to talk. No matter Skyler's tactics in three hours of intense questioning, Ketchum wouldn't tell them about Otto, leaving Cash no choice. He had to tell Krista he'd failed to find her grandfather.

Imagining her disappointment, Cash slid into his car. She had to be frantic for news about Opa.

Odd that she hadn't called to ask about him. Or had she?

Cash checked his phone and found no messages, missed calls or texts. An uneasy feeling tightened his gut. Something could be wrong at the house. He grabbed his phone and dialed

Brady's cell. No answer. He called Krista. After three rings, the call went straight to voice mail.

Cash's radar started wildly pinging.

Maybe Ketchum was telling the truth—someone else was stalking Krista and had abducted Otto. Meaning she could be in danger right now.

Cash fired up the car and bolted from the parking space. On the road, he called Jake and asked him to dispatch the team to Otto's house. After Cash disconnected, he pushed the gas pedal to the floor and careened through the streets at top speed. Fortunately, traffic was light, and he made it to the house in less than fifteen minutes. He parked out of sight on the road and crept through trees toward the building. Shadows played on the ground as the wind jostled branches above, upping his anxiety. He spotted a black SUV parked up close. He checked the license plates.

What? It was the man who'd been watching her—the man who they now knew wasn't the bomber, but Cash didn't know what he was doing here.

Cash eased up to the car. He saw movement and lifted his flashlight to the back window. Lime-green shoes poked out from under a blanket. Otto. It was Otto.

Praying he was healthy, Cash silently opened the back. "Otto, it's me. Cash."

Otto responded with muffled urgency.

Cash removed the blanket and quickly freed Otto. "Can you stand?"

"Yes." He smiled. "It is good to see you, Cash Dixon."

"It's good to see you, too, Otto." Cash smiled back. "Let's get you someplace safe and you can tell me what's going on here."

Cash settled the blanket around Otto and found a secluded spot in the trees. Even with the blanket, Otto shivered. Cash wished he had time to escort Otto to the car, but Krista's life was on the line. Helping the older man down the driveway would waste precious minutes. Cash shrugged out of his jacket and gave it to Otto.

"I cannot take your jacket," Otto said.

"Sure you can." Cash helped Otto into the coat, then draped the blanket on Otto's shoulders. "Now, tell me what's going on."

Otto proceeded to tell a wild tale about his abductor partnering with Toby Alger and killing him. "I do not know this man's name and I never got a look at him, but he is certain Krista has the money. She does not have it. This I know. He is going to kill her if she doesn't tell him where it is."

Cash shook his head. "No, he's not. Not as long as I'm breathing."

TWENTY-THREE

Krista tried to wrench free from Ian's bruising grip, but he held fast and dragged her down steep steps. A cold wind whipped through the trees and cut through her shirt. Ian had taken the time to shrug into one of Opa's jackets hanging on the hook by the door but he'd wanted her to suffer so he denied her a jacket.

"Stop fighting me, Krista." Ian's face was so close she could feel his breath. "You're the only one who's going to get hurt."

"I'm not stupid. I know you won't kill me until you find the money."

He laughed, an ugly, guttural sound. "Doesn't mean I won't make your every remaining moment a nightmare until you talk."

A shiver worked over her body.

"That's right, sweetheart." He laughed again. "You should be afraid."

He stopped for a moment. Listened. She did, too. Heard nothing but the wind. What was he noticing? He suddenly shook his head and continued on, picking up speed.

Her foot hit a rock. She tumbled to the ground, a sharp stick slicing into her cheek. She stifled a cry of distress. She wouldn't give him the satisfaction of hearing her pain.

He jerked her to her feet. His fingers bit like a vise under her elbow, making her wince. They moved closer to the trees lining the river. She heard the water rushing downstream.

Fear threatened to swamp her, and her whole body trembled. He didn't plan to kill her, but the sound of the water reminded her that things could go wrong. Very wrong. She doubted he had any experience with water torture—what if he misjudged how much she could handle before drowning? Or he could lose his hold on her, leaving the river to catch her and sweep her downstream. With her hands tied, she wouldn't be able to swim.

Oh, God, no, she prayed as her heart started pounding.

Cash's face came to mind. She wished he was here with her. To help her, yes, but she desperately wanted to look into his eyes one more time and forget her past. Forget everything and tell him that she'd been wrong to fear her feelings for him. That she loved him. Of that, she was now certain. She needed to survive this ordeal so she could tell him.

Gun drawn, Cash eased up to the family room window. He saw Brady tied to a chair, his hands restrained behind his back and a gag around his mouth. No sign of Krista or the man who'd taken Otto hostage. Cash circled around the house to look in other windows. Nearing the back, he saw a short, stocky man holding a gun to Krista's head and dragging her down the hill by cable ties circling her wrists.

Relief over seeing her alive nearly brought him to his knees. Fear for her safety as the man moved her steadily toward the river instantly replaced it. Cash wanted to bolt after them, but that would be certain death for her. He needed Brady's help. He swung back around the house and charged through the door.

"Otto was in his car. I got him out. He's safe," Cash explained as he removed Brady's gag and cut the ties with his Leatherman. "He told me this guy who has Krista thinks she's got the missing money."

"Guy's name is Ian Summers." Brady cleared his throat. "I'm sorry, man. Krista said he was her husband's friend, or I would never have let him in the house."

"It's not your fault." Cash felt panic threatening to take him down, but he remembered his Delta training, took a few breaths and focused on the problem instead of the people involved. "Let's get a better look at where he's taking Krista and make a plan."

Cash grabbed Otto's bird-watching binoculars on the way out to the deck. He scanned the riverbank, lingering where he saw Summers take Krista into thick scrub. Cash zoomed out to include the water.

"Summers is putting her into a canoe. We need to get onto the water." Cash remembered seeing a small motorboat at the neighbor's house during one of his perimeter checks. He confirmed it was still tied in place, then handed the binoculars to Brady. "Check out the boat. We can use it for a diversion. You head upriver to the boat. I'll swim underwater to Krista and unsettle Summers."

Brady nodded. "With the element of surprise on our side that just might work."

"Let's roll." Cash took the stairs two at a time, Brady right behind him.

On the ground, they wordlessly bumped fists and split up. Cash charged through deep grass toward the water. He'd never been so afraid in his life. Not even when he'd lost his team. That was a sad, sorrow-filled day, but the bomb dropped so quickly Cash had no time to be afraid.

Not today. Today he fought with every breath to keep calm. Their plan had to work. It just had to.

He moved into position and signaled for Brady to fire up the motor. The rumble sounded through the quiet. He gunned the motor, sending the boat winding crazily downstream. Side to side. Back and forth, he made a spectacle of himself.

Summers fixed his attention on Brady just as Cash had planned. He shed his shoes and dived into the water. The cold sapped his breath, but he held a Special Ops Diver badge and had experienced far more difficult conditions. He could easily withstand the temperatures long enough to reach Krista.

He surfaced for a final breath and went back under. He skimmed boulders on the bottom of the river until he caught sight of the canoe above. Careful not to make a sound, he surfaced behind Summers, who sat in the middle of the canoe. Cash gripped the aluminum side with stiff hands and took a few deep breaths. With a sudden burst, he thrust his body up and blindsided Summers, knocking his gun into the river.

"Cash," he heard Krista exclaim before Summers lurched to his feet and turned. He wobbled. The canoe bobbed wildly. Summers lost his balance, tipping over the canoe and ripping it from Cash's hands. Both occupants tumbled into the river.

"No!" Cash shouted as the current quickly carried Krista downriver with her hands still bound.

Summers grabbed for Cash's arm. Cash kneed Summers in the gut. Air hurled from Summers's throat and he let go.

Cash set off after Krista. He pumped his arms. Hand over hand. Stroke after stroke, keeping his eyes on her. She sank, then resurfaced. Sank again.

Father, please, he begged, his muscles burning with fatigue and threatening to seize up.

He focused on his rhythm instead. Kept moving. Pulling hard. Gaining on her bit by bit. She went under again and didn't resurface this time. He dived. Searched through murky water. Found her. Dragged her into his arms and pushed to the surface. He surged higher, lifting her head above water.

She coughed, water spitting from her mouth. She gasped for air and coughed again.

"It's okay, honey," he soothed and trod water as he felt the current pulling them farther downstream. "I've got you. Just relax and breathe."

He wanted to keep talking to her, but a large outcropping of rocks directly ahead caught his attention. With both arms around her, he couldn't fight the current and they'd slam into the rocks.

He looked into her eyes. "I need you to put your legs around my waist and hold on so I can cut your restraints."

"Okay." The word fell from trembling lips.

She wrapped her legs around him, but there was little strength in the muscles.

"Hold tight, honey." He shifted all of her weight to his left arm. The current tried to rip her free, but Cash held fast and retrieved his knife. It took some crazy maneuvering, but he managed to get his Leatherman open and slice the tie. "Can you put your arms around my neck?"

"They're so stiff from being tied and the cold."

She slowly moved her arms, groaning when she brought them up around his neck.

"That's my girl," he said as he heard Brady approaching. He'd fished Summers out of the water and held him down in the boat with a boot lodged in his back.

Brady pulled up next to them and grinned. "Need a ride?"

Cash rolled his eyes and grabbed the boat. "Okay, honey," he said to Krista. "Time to climb in the boat." He maneuvered them so she could grab the edge.

"If you don't want to be a hood ornament for those rocks, you'd best haul yourself into this boat," Brady warned.

The rocks loomed in Cash's peripheral vision. If Brady didn't want to crash the boat and kill all the occupants, he would have to veer the boat sharply away in mere moments and head upstream. Cash couldn't get them both in the boat in time, but he could make sure Krista made it. "We only have one chance at this, honey. I'll give you a push on the count of three, and Brady will grab you, okay?"

She nodded. He counted and shoved, his body submerging under the water until he felt her lift herself over the edge.

He popped up in time to see a massive rock not five feet away. "Go!" he shouted at Brady. "Get us turned around and head upstream. I'll hold on to the side."

Brady gunned the engine and turned the bow in a sudden shift. Cash's arms threatened to wrench from the sockets, but he held fast. The edge of the rock caught his back, tearing his shirt and ripping through his skin.

Krista fell to her knees and grabbed his wrists. She was so weak from the cold and the strain on her arms that she wasn't helping much. But looking into the eyes of the woman he loved, he could do anything. No matter the challenge.

TWENTY-FOUR

One of Cash's hands slipped from the boat.

"Do something, Brady!" Krista screamed. "He's losing his grip."

The boat suddenly stilled. Brady shuffled over her and planted a knee in Ian's back before grabbing Cash's hand at the exact moment his other hand let go. Brady groaned from exertion, but he soon had both of Cash's arms over the edge. He grabbed Cash's belt and hauled him in. Cash fell on top of Ian, who grumbled.

Cash coughed out water, cleared his throat hard and stared at Ian. "I'd like to do a whole lot more than fall on you, buddy. If you don't stop whining, I will." He turned his focus over to his friend. "Get us to the dock, Brady," Cash commanded as he slid back toward Krista.

When he came up beside her, he wrapped an arm around her shoulders and pulled her close. He was chilled to the bone, but just looking at her warmed his soul. "Otto's at the house waiting for you. I found him in Summers's car, and he's fine."

Thank You, God, she prayed and suddenly felt

so blessed. She looked at Cash. "What about Leo Ketchum? Is he the bomber?"

Cash nodded. "He says he didn't ransack your house, though. And obviously he didn't take Otto."

"Ian confessed to breaking in and trashing the house in his search for the money."

"Then it looks like this is all over." He grinned at her. "Just promise me, next time you want to go swimming, you'll wait until summer."

She smiled up at him. "I love that you can joke at a time like this, and I love that you came to my rescue." She touched his cheek that had somehow gotten a nasty scrape in all the action.

He drew her closer. "We have to talk. But not with others around."

"I agree." She scooted closer to him. "A talk is most definitely in order."

At the stairway to the deck at the back of the house, Cash stepped closer to Krista and wrapped his arm around her. He needed to keep touching her as proof that she hadn't been seriously harmed. She snuggled closer. A shock of emotions shot through his body and made his heart soar.

This was right. She was right. *They* were right. So right.

"Hey, Krista," Brady called from behind.

They both turned to look at him as he handed Summers off to a patrol officer.

"I'm sorry," Brady said. "I never should've let this creep in the house."

"We thought he was a friend. You couldn't have known." She smiled. "Besides, you saved my hide in the end and that's all that matters."

"Okay, then." He fired off a salute and they continued up the stairs.

"I didn't know what to think of Brady at first," she said. "But he's starting to grow on me."

Cash glanced back at his buddy. "He doesn't pull any punches even if you want him to, but he's as loyal and dependable as the day is long. I'm proud to call him my friend."

"You've got a lot of friends on your team."

"That I do," he said and decided right then and there that he was done keeping them all at arm's length. Life was just too short not to appreciate and enjoy good people.

The door swung open, and Otto hobbled out. "Liebchen. You are safe. And you, too, Cash." Otto lifted his face to the sky. "Thank You, Father, for Your protection."

Krista threw herself into Otto's arms, nearly knocking him over. Cash couldn't believe she had any strength left. "It was Toby's friend. Ian Summers. He did it. Toby wasn't involved at all."

"I knew my instincts about Toby were right on target." Otto leaned back and smiled at her. "And might I remind you that I told you your judgment was sound all along, and Toby was a good man."

"I should have listened to you."

His smile broadened. "Say that louder, my strong-willed granddaughter, so Cash can hear."

They laughed together, and Cash's heart filled with happiness as he watched them. What a pair. Otto was quite a man, and Krista was an amazing woman. They stood for everything Cash was aching for. A home. Family. Unconditional love and acceptance. Lifelong love and togetherness. He needed those things in his life. Needed Krista. Forever.

A cold wind howled through the woods and whipped across the elevated deck. She shivered.

Cash was over to her in a flash, a protective arm going around her and hugging her close. "We should change into dry clothes."

He escorted her inside and reluctantly released her so she could shower while he did the same thing in Otto's bathroom. After he'd dressed in a pair of scrubs Darcie kept in the rig, he went to the family room. The FRS team had settled in, taking over the small room and making themselves at home. Otto was napping in his bedroom. Hopefully, this episode hadn't damaged his health.

Krista hadn't come out of her room so Cash took a seat on the sofa next to Darcie where he could see Krista the minute she walked in. Veronica was near the door, packing up her equipment, and Brady was explaining to the other FRS team members how Summers had duped Toby.

Cash wondered if learning about Toby's innocence would ease Krista's distrust of men or add to it. Toby hadn't scammed people, but he'd still kept a big secret.

Just as Cash was doing. He had to get time alone with Krista to tell her about his past. Unfortunately, it was looking as if it would take a bomb to get his teammates to leave.

Krista stepped into the room wearing heavy fleece pants and a thick sweatshirt. Her hair was still wet, but her cheeks were rosy.

"Here, take my spot." Cash jumped to his feet and helped her to the sofa. He sat on the arm, staying as close to her as he could. All eyes were on Krista, and it wasn't hard to see how uncomfortable she felt.

She lifted her chin and pulled back her shoulders. "Someone might as well come out and say what you're all thinking."

"Where's the money?" Brady said with his usual grin.

She wrinkled her nose at him. "Of course it would be you to speak first."

"You can always count on Brady for that." Darcie winked at him. "But we love him anyway."

"So-o-o." He fixed his gaze on Krista. "About the money."

Krista slid to the edge of the sofa as if uncertain where she should start.

"Hey, sweetie," Darcie rushed in. "Don't freak

out. We don't think you took it. We're just wondering what you think Toby did with it."

"I have no idea."

"If it was so easy to locate, the detectives would have found it," Skyler said.

Chewing on her lip, Veronica approached them. "I hope you don't mind, but I have an idea."

"Go on," Jake suggested.

She gestured at the desk in the corner with a computer and laser printer. "Was Toby tech savvy?"

Krista nodded. "He kept up on all the latest trends, but Ian told me he already searched the computer." She shivered and clutched her arms around her waist.

Cash hated seeing her suffer from the memory. He squeezed her shoulder. She looked at him and smiled. Soft, sweet and—dare he hope—trusting?

Veronica took a step closer. "Maybe what you're looking for isn't in the computer. Maybe it's in the printer."

"I don't understand," Krista said. "You think there's a jam or something? But it wouldn't work then, would it?"

"I'm not talking about paper. It's not common knowledge, but many laser printers have internal hard drives. The drive writes images of items that have been scanned, printed or copied to the hard drive."

"If Toby knew that," Skyler said excitedly, "he

might have copied a page that gave the location of the money."

"Sounds brilliant to me," Darcie said. "No one would think to look there, right?"

"Um, Darcie." Brady grinned. "Veronica just did."

She swatted a hand at him. "Obviously no one thought to look in the last four years."

"Can you check it out, Veronica?" Krista asked.

"Yes, but not here. We'll have to take the printer in where we can image the hard drive first."

"Like you did with the flash drive?" Cash asked.

She nodded. "But before you get excited, not all printers have a hard drive." She pulled out her phone. "If you give me a minute, I can find the specifications for this one online."

All eyes remained on Veronica. Time ticked by slowly and everyone sat quietly in anticipation. Even Brady's foot had stilled.

She looked up from her phone with a smile. "We're in luck. It has a hard drive."

"Great. I'll ride in with Veronica and put a rush on this." Jake stood and looked at the other team members. "You'll need to take the truck. I don't care who drives, but you'd better bring the rig home in one piece." He tossed the keys in the air. Darcie snatched them and the guys glared at her.

Skyler tugged Darcie up and took her spot next to Krista. "I know you don't want to relive all of this, but I should take your statement while it's fresh in your mind. If you'll give me a sec, I'll call Logan for a ride home, then we can get started."

"The rest of us will get out of your hair." Brady crossed the room and stood looking down on Krista. "I was wrong about you, Krista, and I'm not embarrassed to admit it. I thought my friend here wasn't thinking clearly." He clapped Cash on the back. "Turns out, I was the one who was missing the obvious."

"Not a stretch for you," Cash said, earning a punch in the arm from Brady.

Archer focused on Krista. "Don't be surprised if you have some lingering emotional issues from today. I'd be glad to refer you to someone if you need some help."

"He's right," Darcie added. "No one will think less of you."

Krista smiled. "I appreciate your concern."

"C'mon, you two," Darcie said to Brady and Archer. "First one to the truck gets to drive."

The guys bolted for the door, and Cash laughed. "It's not often Jake lets anyone else drive."

"I'm sorry I'm missing out on it." Skyler pulled her micro-recorder from her pocket. "Let's get started with your statement, Krista."

Cash didn't miss the fact that Skyler had stopped using Ms. Curry. A big step for her.

Krista started her story and stayed strong like the trouper she'd proved to be. Cash, however, nearly lost it as Krista described Ian's rough treatment. An hour later, Skyler was wrapping up the questions when her phone rang.

"It's Jake," she said, then put him on speaker.

"Are you all sitting down?" he asked.

Could mean good or bad news and Cash had had it with the bad stuff. "Just tell us what you found."

"We not only have the banking information, but a spreadsheet Toby copied the night he died. It lists every scammed senior and the amount of money they lost."

"That's wonderful," Krista exclaimed. "We can pay them back."

"I'm sure there will be a bunch of legal mumbo jumbo to go through, but yeah, looks like the victims will be getting their money back. And you'll be happy to know, Summers has made a full confession."

"Then Krista is completely in the clear." Skyler smiled at Krista. "I hope you're not upset that we had to keep you on our suspect list."

"Honestly, I was worried you were like Detective Eason, but you're nothing like him." Krista squeezed Skyler's hand.

"If you girls are done kissing and making up..." Jake's voice came over the phone as the doorbell rang.

"That will be Logan." Skyler got up. "Do you need anything else, Jake?"

"Nah. Go spend time with Logan. You worked hard on this investigation and you've earned it."

She disconnected. "Well, you heard the man. I've been ordered to spend time with my sweetie." Laughing, she headed for the door, then turned. "FYI, Krista, I'll be calling Eason. We'll hold a joint press conference to make sure everyone knows your name is cleared."

"Which means I can go back to my legal name." Krista smiled.

"That you can." Skyler stepped out the door.

Cash dropped onto the sofa next to Krista. "Alone at last."

She peered at him. "I'm really starting to like your teammates, but I was hoping they'd leave."

He took her hand, closing his fingers around hers. His hand dwarfed hers, her skin soft. Her lips curved in a shaky smile, bringing out dimples he hadn't seen before. The phone rang.

"Let it roll to the answering machine," Cash urged as he moved even closer.

She didn't get up to answer, but despite Cash's efforts to keep her attention, she kept her gaze fixed on the machine. Disappointed, Cash cupped the side of her face to get her attention. She focused on him until the caller announced that he was Otto's doctor wanting to report Otto's latest test results. She jumped up and grabbed the phone, catching the doctor before he hung up.

"You have the results?" she whispered, as if afraid to hear the news.

Cash saw her pull in a breath and hold it. He did the same thing. Waiting. Hoping. Watching.

She listened intently until a wide smile slid across her face. She thanked the doctor, and as she hung up, she twirled in a circle, her eyes alight with happiness.

"Good news, I take it," Cash said.

"Opa's responding to the chemo. The doctor is optimistic about his prognosis."

"That's great." Cash's heart flooded with joy.

Krista sat but instead of seeming open to him, she hugged her arms around herself.

Was she protecting herself from him? From the chance of being hurt by another man?

When he finally explained that he'd kept something from her, would she walk away?

He drew in a breath to tell her, but all of a sudden he wasn't certain he was strong enough to take the risk.

Something changed in Cash. He'd been alive and cheerful, as happy for Opa as Krista was, then suddenly the light had gone out as if someone had flipped a switch. She had to know what was going on.

She made sure her gaze was soft and encouraging. "You can tell me whatever's bothering you."

He opened his mouth. Closed it. Opened it

again. "I...I've been thinking. About all you've gone through lately. Men have let you down a lot. Except Otto."

She hadn't expected this topic at all, but she'd go with it. "I've had my share of disappointments. That's why I didn't want to get involved with anyone. I kept saying it was because I couldn't trust my own judgment, but honestly, I was just afraid of getting hurt again."

"I'll never hurt you," he said almost in a whisper. "At least not intentionally." He took her hand, engulfing it with long, strong fingers. "I'm not really keeping a secret from you like Toby did, but there's a part of my life I haven't told you about."

A moment of apprehension had her drawing back, but she was done running. If he revealed something horrible, she'd find a way to deal with it. "Tell me."

"When I was Delta...my team...we were family, you know? But then, one day...it was near Kandahar. We were charged with escorting a special leader and keeping him alive at all costs. There was this bridge." He stopped and shook his head, his sorrow so obvious she knew something terrible was coming.

"Once we crossed the bridge, we'd be home free. But then the Taliban attacked. Had us pinned down. Our only way out was to call in air support. It was risky because we were so close to the insurgents. A two-thousand-pound bomb falling that close…I don't have to tell you what it could do, but it was our only option. I was the senior officer so I made the call."

He paused again and she felt him tremble. She clutched his hand and willed him the strength to go on.

"The bomb went astray." He looked up at the ceiling. "I'll never forget it hitting. I was thrown in the air and my ears started ringing. Chaos all around me. The only thing that saved me was the mud walls. They'd baked in the hot sun for so long they took the worst of the blast." His voice dropped lower. "The other guys on the team didn't make it. I had a blown eardrum and a knot on my head, but that was it. I was fine. Our protectee survived. Mission accomplished. But the cost. Man, the cost."

"I'm so sorry, Cash," she said and knew her words couldn't possibly convey how badly she felt for him. "You must've been devastated."

He jerked his hand free and plunged it into his hair. "I shouldn't be walking around talking about it while the guys are buried six feet under."

"You couldn't have done anything to stop it."

"I know, and here's the thing. I've thought about it and thought about it. Over and over, replaying the day. And every time I come up with the same thing. If I was in that position today, I'd do the same thing. The odds of a bomb going astray?

Let's just say they're crazy big odds. I made the right call."

"But it still hurts."

"Yeah, and I gotta wonder, why me, you know? Why'd I survive? God could've let me go, too. Some days I think it would've been easier."

"Please don't think that way. Ever." She grabbed his hand again and kissed the palm. "God wants you alive, and He put you in my life. Maybe to save me like you tried to do with your men. To save the other people you've rescued in your new job. To let me see I can trust men again. To love again." She looked deeply into his eyes. "I love you, Cash. With my whole heart."

He flashed a quick smile, one that made his whole face come alive.

"I love you, too," he said but his smile fell. "But you have to know. This thing with my team and the way it makes me feel…I'm working on it, but I haven't resolved it. Still, seeing what you and Otto share gives me hope I can have the same thing in my life."

"You want to be my grandfather?" she joked to lighten the tension.

"Most definitely not your grandfather." He gave her a wicked look, jerked her into his arms and kissed her soundly.

"Hmm," she said when he lifted his head. "That kiss was not at all grandfatherly."

He trailed his finger down her cheek and that

luminous smile returned. A smile that made her feel as if she was the only person in his life. A smile she'd love to have trained on her again and again.

"Maybe we should try it again," he said. "Like a thousand or so times and then come up for air."

"I'm thinking Opa might come out before that happens. But then again, he probably wouldn't interrupt. You passed the Opa test long ago."

"Is that so?"

She nodded solemnly. "Very few people make the cut, so we better get started on that relationship before we disappoint him."

Cash smiled. "I agree, Krista Cu—Alger."

She frowned. "You're going to have to get used to the different last name."

"Not to worry." The same grin lit his face. "I suspect it won't be long before you'll have another name change. I kinda like Krista Dixon. How about you?"

"Oh, yeah." She gazed into his eyes, her heart overflowing with love. "Krista Dixon sounds perfect to me."

* * * * *

Dear Reader,

Peace. It's such an elusive concept at times. At least it is for me. I'm a take-charge kind of person and when things don't go according to plan, I sometimes lose my peace. It's at these times I have to step back and ask God what His plans are in this situation. If I don't, I will fret until the problem is resolved.

Though I consciously work on this area in my own life, I still struggle with it. That's why I decided to write the First Responder series. Each story revolves around finding peace in trying times. In fact, as I wrote book two, *Explosive Alliance*, I was surprised at how much the spiritual content applied to my life. I hope as you read this series and see the team members search for peace in their lives that they will help you find more peace in yours.

If you'd like to learn more about this new series, stop by my website at susansleeman.com. I also love hearing from readers, so please contact me via email, susan@susansleeman.com, on my Facebook page, facebook.com/SusanSleemanBooks, or write to me at Love Inspired, 233 Broadway, Suite 1001, New York, NY 10279.

Susan Sleeman

LARGER-

GET 2 FREE
LARGER-PRINT NOV
PLUS 2 FREE
MYSTERY GIFTS

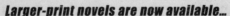

Larger-print novels are now available...

YES! Please send me 2 FREE LARGER-PRINT Love Inspired® novels and my 2 FREE mystery gifts (gifts are worth about $10). After receiving them, if I don't wish to receive any more books, I can return the shipping statement marked "cancel." If I don't cancel, I will receive 6 brand-new novels every month and be billed just $5.49 per book in the U.S. or $5.99 per book in Canada. That's a savings of at least 19% off the cover price. It's quite a bargain! Shipping and handling is just 50¢ per book in the U.S. and 75¢ per book in Canada.* I understand that accepting the 2 free books and gifts places me under no obligation to buy anything. I can always return a shipment and cancel at any time. Even if I never buy another book, the two free books and gifts are mine to keep forever.

122/322 IDN GH6D

Name	(PLEASE PRINT)	
Address		Apt. #
City	State/Prov.	Zip/Postal Code

Signature (if under 18, a parent or guardian must sign)

Mail to the **Reader Service:**
IN U.S.A.: P.O. Box 1867, Buffalo, NY 14240-1867
IN CANADA: P.O. Box 609, Fort Erie, Ontario L2A 5X3

**Are you a current subscriber to Love Inspired® books
and want to receive the larger-print edition?
Call 1-800-873-8635 or visit www.ReaderService.com.**

* Terms and prices subject to change without notice. Prices do not include applicable taxes. Sales tax applicable in N.Y. Canadian residents will be charged applicable taxes. Offer not valid in Quebec. This offer is limited to one order per household. Not valid to current subscribers to Love Inspired Larger-Print books. All orders subject to credit approval. Credit or debit balances in a customer's account(s) may be offset by any other outstanding balance owed by or to the customer. Please allow 4 to 6 weeks for delivery. Offer available while quantities last.

Your Privacy—The Reader Service is committed to protecting your privacy. Our Privacy Policy is available online at www.ReaderService.com or upon request from the Reader Service.

We make a portion of our mailing list available to reputable third parties that offer products we believe may interest you. If you prefer that we not exchange your name with third parties, or if you wish to clarify or modify your communication preferences, please visit us at www.ReaderService.com/consumerchoice or write to us at Reader Service Preference Service, P.O. Box 9062, Buffalo, NY 14240-9062. Include your complete name and address.

LILP15